Surrounded

Just when Emily thought she might collapse from all the wild dancing with Ben, the lights in the ballroom dimmed, and the band went into a slow, dreamy number.

"May I?"

Emily turned around to see Scott holding out his hand, and a tiny gasp of surprise escaped her lips. Her instinct was to stay away from him, but like a magnet, she found herself drawn into his outstretched arms. She couldn't fight it, and sliding her arms around his waist, she leaned her head on his shoulder. For a moment they simply stood there, holding each other and letting the soft music surround them.

Books from Scholastic
in the **Couples** series:

Couples Special Editions

Summer Heat!
Be Mine!

SLOW DANCING

M.E. Cooper

SCHOLASTIC INC.
New York Toronto London Auckland Sydney

ISBN 0-590-40427-X

12 11 10 9 8 7 6 5 4 3 2 1   7 8 9/8 0 1 2/9

Printed in the U.S.A.   01

First Scholastic printing, May 1987

SLOW DANCING

Chapter
1

Emily Stevens took a deep breath as she jogged along the gravel path in Rose Hill Park. It was a perfect day for a run in the park — cool and clear, without a trace of wind — and Emily loved jogging. She also loved living in Rose Hill. After spending two-and-a-half years at boarding school while her father, a diplomat with the State Department, was assigned to South America, she was thrilled to be living at home again.

Her parents had bought an old Victorian house when her father was reassigned to Washington, D.C., just before Christmas. And when Emily came home for vacation, they had told her she would be transferring to Kennedy High at the end of the semester. It was the best Christmas present ever. She had liked Middlecroft and had made some good friends there, but she had also missed seeing her parents every day and having a room of her own.

Now she had them both. And she had made new friends at Kennedy. She had worried at first about starting a new high school in the middle of her junior year, but she had been accepted by the crowd immediately and just as quickly gained a reputation as someone fellow students could turn to for advice.

"Hi! Mind if I run along with you for a while?" A male voice sounded beside her, and Emily started. She hadn't heard anyone approach.

Brushing aside a strand of hair which had fallen over her eyes, she looked over to see a tall, slim boy with broad shoulders straining against a red and gold Kennedy High T-shirt, and a ruggedly handsome face. Sandy blond hair fell over his forehead, and his eyes were a blue-gray, she noticed, as he looked at her uncertainly.

"Sure," Emily said. "In fact, I'd like company. Makes the run easier."

The boy smiled. "You look like you're doing okay to me." There was no teasing in his voice.

Emily smiled at him and glanced at her digital watch. It flashed eighteen minutes. She was averaging about a nine-minute mile. "Are you sure I'm not going too slowly for you?"

"Nope," the boy replied. "The pace is perfect. I always run too fast when I'm alone."

Emily nodded, acutely aware of his long legs moving rhythmically beside hers. There was something so graceful about the way he ran, she sensed he'd be comfortable at any speed.

"Uh . . . by the way, my name is Scott Phillips. I'm a junior at Kennedy." His eyes roved questioningly over her face. "Haven't I seen you around school?"

Emily turned to him, her blue eyes wide. "You might have. I'm a junior, too."

"I thought you looked familiar," his eyes examined the smooth oval of her face again before sweeping quickly over her slender figure in pink-and-white striped jogging shorts and matching pink T-shirt.

"What did you say your name was?"

"I'm sorry, I didn't," she answered. "I'm Emily Stevens."

Scott's face lit up when he smiled. "Nice to meet you, Emily." He reached over a hand and somehow managed to enclose hers.

The instant their hands touched, Emily felt a tingle go up her spine. She turned her eyes to meet Scott's, and forgot to concentrate on where she was running. She didn't see the rut in the jogging path.

"Oops!" she cried out as she felt herself stumble. She flung an arm out in front of her to stop her fall but before she knew what was happening, she felt a strong arm close securely around her waist.

"You okay?" Scott asked once he had set her back on her feet, and they both took a moment to catch their breaths.

Emily looked over to see his blue-gray eyes looking at her with concern, and she nodded. "Leave it to me to find the one rut in the jogging path."

Scott laughed. "Yeah. But at least it's behind us now."

They resumed their steady pace up a long, winding hill, and Emily tried not to let him see she was beginning to struggle. She hated running up hills and might have avoided this one entirely if she hadn't been running with Scott.

"Nice view, isn't it?" he said, once they reached the top of the hill, and the jogging path flattened out.

Emily could only nod. She was now entirely out of breath, but the struggle had been worth it. The view *was* spectacular. Below the grassy slopes of the park was the Potomac River — wide and blue, with only an occasional ripple of white. And at this time of year it was especially breathtaking. Thick foliage bordered its banks, and now that everything was in bloom, the river formed a perfect backdrop for the colorful beds of crocus and rhododendron that dotted the park.

"That's it for me," she told him reluctantly, once they had completed a loop around the park. "Right now, five miles is my limit."

"You did great," he said, as she started to slow her pace. "Want to run together again sometime?"

Emily felt her pulse quicken. "Sure," she said. "Whenever you want. I run practically every afternoon."

"How about weekends?"

"Sometimes." She didn't want to appear too eager. "But usually in the morning."

"No problem," Scott said before continuing along the running path. "See you at school."

On the way home, Emily tried to think of the history paper she still had to type, but her mind would not budge beyond thoughts of Scott. It was hard to believe that in the five months she'd been at Kennedy High, she had never noticed him. He was not only good-looking, but more important, he had an easy, warm personality that made her feel comfortable the moment they met. He was easy to talk to and hadn't gone out of his way to impress her like some boys she knew. When Emily pictured his blue-gray eyes and shock of blond hair, she got a warm feeling all over.

"Hey, Emily, wait! I've got to talk to you!"

She looked up and saw Elise Hammond pulling her car into the driveway. She'd been so preoccupied with thoughts of Scott, she hadn't realized she was in front of her friend's house.

"Hi, Elise. What's up?" she asked.

Elise shook her curly dark hair away from her face and hurriedly climbed out of the car to open the trunk. Inside was a large white box, but before she reached in to lift it out, she gave a furtive glance over her shoulder. Emily was used to her friend's sense of drama, but the way she was carrying on right now was definitely weird. She looked as if she was afraid someone was going to jump out of the bushes.

Emily stared at her, puzzled. "Is something wrong?"

"Sh-h-h-h." Elise motioned for her to be quiet, and hurried her into the house. "I don't want Ben to see me with the box."

Ben was Elise's boyfriend, and he happened to live directly across the street from her. But that didn't explain why she wanted to keep the box a secret.

"Made it!" sighed Elise, leaning against the closed door. By now Emily was bursting with curiosity. It was definitely time to find out what was going on.

She followed her friend upstairs to the privacy of her bedroom and plopped down on the bed. "Okay, enough already. What is *in* there?" she asked, pointing to the box Elise still held clutched in her hands.

"You remember the dress we saw last week when we went to the Rose Hill Mall?" Elise asked as she walked over to the bed and set down the box. "The green one, with the shoulder ties and tiered skirt?"

"Mm-hmmmm." Emily nodded. They had agreed it would make a gorgeous prom dress.

"Well . . . I went back to the mall and bought it. Do you think I'm wacko?"

Emily laughed. "Of course I think you're wacko. But not because you bought the dress. It really *was* gorgeous."

She watched Elise lift the dress from the box and hold it in front of her. She preened self-consciously in front of the mirror.

"Why do you want to keep the dress a secret from Ben?" she asked. "Don't you think he's going to like it?"

"He may never get to see it," Elise sighed as she slumped down onto the bed.

Elise stared at her friend. "What? Be serious!"

"I am being serious. That's what I wanted to talk to you about. I need advice."

"Okay then. Go on," Emily prompted. "I'm listening."

"Everyone's been talking about the prom for weeks. In fact it's *all* anyone's been talking about. Well, I told Dee and Fiona that Ben and I would sit at the same table with them. But the truth is, I'm not even sure I'll be going to the prom." Elise looked as though she might cry.

For a moment Emily was speechless. Elise made it sound like she and Ben were on the verge of breaking up. "Did you have a fight?" she asked.

"No. It's nothing like that," Elise sighed. "It's just that Ben still hasn't asked me to the prom."

Emily looked at her friend, unable to hide her disbelief. This was completely out of character for Elise. She'd always been the take-charge type, especially when it came to Ben.

"Elise Hammond," she chided her playfully, "you really are a complete wacko. Don't you remember what Ben was like the last time he got involved in a new science project? He probably just forgot to ask you."

Elise smiled weakly. "You really think so?"

"Yes, I really think so," Emily said, placing her arm around her friend. "What other reason could there be?" She expected Elise to laugh then, but the expression on Elise's face remained pained.

"So what am I supposed to do?"

To Emily the solution was so obvious she was surprised Elise hadn't thought of it herself. "Simple," she said, giving her friend's hand a supportive squeeze. "*You* ask *him* to the prom."

Elise laughed a little then. "Of course. Why didn't I think of that?"

"You would have, given enough time," Emily assured her as she stood up, arching her back. She hadn't done any stretching exercises after her run this afternoon and her muscles were beginning to tighten up.

"Thanks a lot, Em," said Elise, standing up to give her a hug. "You really are the Kennedy High 'Dear Abby.'"

"If you don't need me anymore," Emily said, bending over to touch her toes, "I'm going home. I still have a history paper to type."

"That reminds me," Elise said slapping the palm of her hand against her forehead. "Jonathan Preston, the student activities director, asked me to make a few calls for him this afternoon. He thought it would be nice if the junior class did something special for the graduating seniors, and he's trying to arrange a brainstorming session in the student activities room tomorrow during lunch. How about it? Will you come?"

"Sure," Emily agreed, resting her head against her knees. "Who else is going to be there?" She almost came out and asked about Scott, but caught herself at the last second.

"Most of the junior crowd, I guess," Elise told her.

Emily straightened up and felt her cheeks flush. Did that include Scott? She felt the by-now familiar rush of warmth she got whenever she remembered the way he had looked at her, or the gentle pressure of his strong arm about her waist.

"By the way, I met this guy jogging today. He says he's a junior at Kennedy, but I've never seen him before."

"What's his name?" Elise asked. "Maybe I know him."

"Scott Phillips."

Elise hung her new dress in the closet and turned to face Emily. "Sure, I know Scott. He sits next to me in English. How'd you meet jogging?"

"We just happened to meet on the path and decided to pace each other."

Elise giggled. "Don't tell that to Heather Richardson. She'd die of envy."

Emily looked at her friend, not sure she understood.

"She's Scott's girl friend," Elise said. "At least I think she is. He's been riding around in her car an awful lot lately."

Emily said nothing. Everyone, even someone relatively new to Kennedy like herself, knew who Heather Richardson was. She was one of the most visible people in the whole school. A real show-off, Heather loved to flaunt her family's wealth by parking her burgundy BMW in front of school, instead of in the student parking lot. She also wore flashy clothes that clung revealingly to her well-rounded figure, and when she spoke, she managed to drown out everyone around her. She was in Emily's biology class, and whenever she walked into the room, people noticed. She was a tremendous flirt, too. But Heather and Scott? Suddenly the lightheartedness went out of Emily's day.

Chapter
2

The first thing Emily saw when she arrived at school the next morning was Heather's burgundy BMW. As usual, it was parked directly in front of Kennedy High for everyone to see.

Emily pulled the hood of her yellow rain slicker closer around her head and spun around toward the quad. She didn't care that the grass was wet and dotted with puddles of water. It was faster to sidestep them than to walk around the quad to the main building. It was also a way to avoid passing in front of Heather's car.

She still found it hard to believe that Scott and Heather were a couple. Somehow it didn't make sense. Thinking back to how unpretentious Scott had appeared yesterday, Emily couldn't picture him falling for someone like Heather Richardson. He was so reserved compared to her. But he was also attractive enough to date any girl he wanted to at Kennedy High. Emily wasn't foolish enough to believe she was the first girl to ever develop a crush on Scott. With his looks and that smile, he'd probably been breaking hearts for years.

But life was full of the unexpected, Emily told herself as she jumped over another puddle. Hadn't the weatherman forecast sun for today? Yet the air was thick with moisture and a steady drizzle fell. Emily wasn't going to let herself believe that things were already over with Scott before they'd even started. After all, she hadn't developed a reputation as the school's "Dear Abby" for nothing.

She took a deep breath and shrugged. She didn't want to think about Scott anymore this morning. Instead, she forced herself to concentrate on avoiding the few remaining puddles until she reached the side entrance to the school.

Pulling open the wide double doors, she was enveloped by an earsplitting roar, as the hordes of students in the crowded corridor shouted to be heard above the clanging of locker doors. Emily waited for a moment before weaving her way through the mass of bodies. Her locker was at the far end of the wide corridor, but she was in no real hurry to get there. She even stopped a moment to chat with a girl from her history class, and took her time greeting everyone with a smile and a wave.

When she finally did reach her locker, she dropped her book bag by her feet and slowly began dialing her locker combination.

"Hi." Jonathan Preston leaned over to tap her on the shoulder. "I'm looking for Elise. Have you seen her around?"

11

Emily pulled open her locker door before glancing around to see him standing behind her. "Oh, hi, Jonathan." She smiled and shrugged out of her jacket. "If I know Elise, she'll come charging in at the last minute as usual. But if you want to leave a message, her locker's over there," she said, pointing across the corridor.

"Thanks."

He wasn't aware that Fiona Stone was heading toward them until she stopped beside him and slid her arm through his. Fiona was a sophomore whose family had moved to Rose Hill from England at the beginning of the school year. She and Jonathan had been going out since just before Christmas.

"Hi, Em," Fiona said in her British accent. "You going to be at the meeting this afternoon?"

Jonathan gave her a glance that said, "Keep your voice down." He turned back to face Emily. "Will you tell Elise that I spoke to Mr. Barker, our class adviser, about what we intend to do and that the meeting's all set to take place during lunch?"

"Oh?" It took a moment for Emily to recall what he was talking about.

"And try not to mention anything about it in front of the seniors," he added as the warning bell rang. "We want to keep it a secret — at least for now."

Emily nodded. "Sure, no problem."

"Okay then! We'll see you later. I've still got to catch three more people before the final bell. Are you coming?" he looked at Fiona.

"You sure you want me to?"

12

"What kind of question is that?"

"You know what I mean. I might say the wrong thing again."

"You're always saying the wrong thing." He wrapped his arms around her waist. "But I love you just the same."

"Well, if you put it that way, how can I resist? I'll see you at the meeting," Fiona whispered to Emily before Jonathan dragged her away.

And as they moved down the hall, Jonathan with his Indiana Jones hat perched awkwardly on his head, and Fiona looking every bit the ballerina that she was, Emily had to smile. Despite their constant arguing they were really very happy together. She remembered hearing how rigid and miserable Fiona had been when she first came to Kennedy from England. She wasn't dancing then, and Fiona was born to dance. It was Jonathan who convinced her of that, and encouraged her to enroll in a professional ballet school. Now, instead of that hard edge, Fiona had a softness about her that brought out her natural grace and improved her personality.

Emily leaned down to open her book bag and pulled out her history paper to read once more before handing it in. As she stood up, Elise came dashing up to her locker.

"Emily, you'll never guess what just happened!" she exclaimed. She was so excited, she was bouncing on her toes.

"In that case, you'd better tell me." Emily smiled at her friend.

"I can't . . . I mean, I want you to guess."

"Okay." Emily hesitated, pretending to be

deep in thought. "Your sister called from college last night to say she's getting married."

Elise giggled. "Don't be ridiculous. She just broke up with her boyfriend!"

"You're getting married!"

Elise giggled again. "Not quite. But you're getting warm."

"I am?" Emily shrugged. She couldn't imagine what else would get Elise so excited. "Can't you at least give me a hint?"

"Nope."

"Come on, Be a pal," Emily pleaded. "The bell's going to ring any second now, and I still have to look over my history paper."

"All right." Elise weakened. "But only one clue." She leaned over and whispered, "It has to do with Ben."

"Ben?" Emily exclaimed. "What did he do, win the National Science Award? Or better yet, decide to give up science altogether?"

"Neither. He asked me to the prom this morning," Elise answered breathlessly. "Here we are standing in the rain on the corner of Everett Street, waiting for the other kids to show up, and he just pops out with it."

Emily laughed. "I hope you said yes."

Suddenly Elise's face grew serious. "I told him I would have to think about it."

"You what!" Emily shouted. She rarely raised her voice, but this was too much — especially after the way Elise had carried on yesterday with the prom dress. "What was there to think about?"

"Nothing, but I couldn't let *him* know that." She said, and began shrugging out of her raincoat.

14

Emily was at a loss for words. Only Elise would dare pull a stunt like that. "Exactly when do you plan on letting him know you'll be going?" she asked, staring directly into her friend's eyes.

Emily wondered if Elise knew how lucky she was to have a guy like Ben. Not every boy would be willing to put up with her craziness.

"Oh, I already did," said Elise, heading across the hallway to her locker. "As soon as we got to school."

Emily gave her friend a mock-dirty look, and turned back to her locker to check over her history paper. There were times she would have liked to strangle Elise.

The final bell rang, and a mass of frantic bodies started scrambling toward the stairwells. Emily quickly gathered up her books and was closing her locker door when Elise came over and gave her arm a squeeze.

"Don't you touch me, Ms. Manipulator!" Emily jerked away. But there was a big grin on her face.

Elise saw it and slung her arm around Emily's shoulder instead. "By the way, I bumped into Jonathan when I was coming into school," she told her as they started for the stairs. "He mentioned the meeting was all set for lunch."

As Emily neared the student activities room she felt her nerves grow jittery. It was crazy, but she couldn't help herself. The thought that she might see Scott again sent her stomach flip-flopping. All morning she'd been unable to get him out of her thoughts. Even after she promised herself she wouldn't think about him anymore, she still found him intruding upon the usually organized progression of her life. It was bad enough he'd been on her mind all last night while she'd been trying to concentrate on typing her paper, but this morning when Mr. Baylor had called on her to read it in front of the class, she'd been thinking of Scott and hadn't heard him. Mr. Baylor had to repeat her name twice before she snapped out of her daydream, and by then the entire class was laughing.

Her footsteps slowed, and when she reached the water fountain, stopped altogether. Right now the corridor was filled with students heading toward the lunchroom. Maybe she should just follow them instead of going to the meeting. She patted her stomach to ease the butterflies. The idea tempted her, but only for a moment. More than anything, Emily wanted to see Scott, and she knew it was likely he'd be at the meeting.

She darted into the bathroom to comb her hair before heading into the student activities room, and found herself staring at her image and wondering what Scott had thought when he'd first seen her. She wasn't beautiful like Diana Einerson, who could make a living as a model. But Emily was satisfied with the way she looked. She had a nicely shaped face, with dark hair, large blue eyes, and dark eyebrows. Her figure, too, was okay, Emily thought. She had slender, muscular legs from jogging regularly. She wasn't as tall as she might like to be, but she thought her proportions were just right.

She snapped out of her reverie, and quickly smoothed her oversized striped shirt down over her jeans. Emily didn't want to be late for the meeting. She had only meant to take a quick look in the mirror, but somehow everything she did today made her think of Scott.

She ran to the door before the butterflies could come back and stepped into the hallway. At that same moment Woody Webster came bouncing around the corner. Emily knew that Woody prided himself on knowing everything that was going on at Kennedy High, and guessed it was no accident he happened to be coming from the direction of the student activities room just then. Behind the clown's exterior he presented to everyone, he was pretty clever.

"Hiya, Emily. What's cooking?" he asked, bouncing up to her, with his thumbs hooked in a pair of yellow plaid suspenders. "I just passed the student activities room and understand there's a big meeting about to take place — juniors only. How come? Aren't you going to need any expert advice?" His eyes twinkled.

Emily smiled. "Not this time, Woody. But thanks for offering."

Woody shook his head. "Where's your feeling of togetherness? Your school spirit?" He started singing the Kennedy High Fight Song.

Emily burst into laughter. "Don't you ever give up?" she asked.

Woody immediately stopped singing and dropped his head in mock self-pity. "I know. You don't think I'm good enough for your crowd."

"Enough!" Emily groaned. "The only thing wrong with you, Woody Webster, besides being nosy, is that you're a senior. Now if you'll excuse

17

me, I've got a meeting to attend." She skirted past him and started down the hall.

"Okay, have it your way. Just remember I offered," he called after her. "You know where to find me if you should change your mind," he added, backing off down the corridor.

Emily nodded without looking back, and willed her feet to move faster. Most likely everyone who was coming to the meeting was already there, including Scott.

The moment she walked in, she heard someone call her name. She looked around to see who it was. Diana Einerson was sitting at the far end of the conference table next to Jeremy Stone, Fiona's brother.

"I've saved a seat for you." Diana motioned for Emily to join them.

Other members of the junior class were already seated around the table. Dee Patterson was showing her boyfriend Marc some of the photographs she'd taken for *The Red and the Gold*, the school newspaper. Next to her Karen Davis, a real brain who hosted the WKND news show, was talking to Pamela Green. Emily had met Pam a couple of months ago when she worked on the student art show, and she liked her a lot. She was a terrific artist and taught art classes at Garfield House, a halfway house for teenagers in Georgetown where many of the Kennedy students did volunteer work.

Emily moved past Ben, who had his nose in a book as usual, and headed toward one of the empty chairs. Jonathan Preston nodded to her. He was wearing his felt Indiana Jones hat, and his friendly gray eyes seemed to welcome her.

Standing at the front of the room with him was Matt Jacobs, and Emily overheard Matt telling Jonathan that Brian Pierson, the new music DJ, wouldn't be at the meeting. Scott wasn't there, either, which meant he probably wasn't coming.

She tried to squelch the disappointment welling up inside as she pulled out a chair and sat down beside Diana. Although she was dying to know if Scott had even been told about the meeting, she didn't feel comfortable asking.

"I'm glad so many people showed up," Emily said.

"Me, too." Diana smiled. "Especially since most kids would rather spend their lunch hour goofing off than sitting in a meeting."

Then it occurred to her. How could she have thought Scott would be at the meeting when he could be with Heather in the lunchroom? She could picture them sitting side by side at one of the long tables, huddled close and sharing lunches, like all the other couples at Kennedy High.

With sagging spirits, Emily reached into her book bag and pulled out a sandwich. She really didn't feel like eating, but she knew she'd never make it through the afternoon if she didn't.

"Hey, that looks good," a resonant male voice said from behind her.

Emily whirled around, her heart thumping. Scott Phillips was leaning against the back of the chair next to hers, and smiling. She could make out the faintest hint of a dimple in his left cheek.

"What are you doing here?" Emily managed to find her voice but the minute the words were past her lips she felt silly for having asked such a rude question.

Scott didn't seem to mind. "I'm a junior, too," he said. "Don't you remember me? We jogged together yesterday?"

Remember him! If only he knew he was all she'd been thinking about for the past twenty-four hours. Seeing him here now made her feel delightfully light-headed. If possible, he looked even better dressed in faded jeans and an old blue work shirt than he had in his jogging clothes.

He pulled out the chair next to her and sat down, sending Emily's pulse racing double-time.

Chapter
3

Elise burst into the student activities room. "Sorry I'm late. I had to stop off in the lunchroom for yogurt. Did I miss anything?"

"Just some gossip," Ben teased, having looked up from the book he was reading when he heard her voice.

"Really? Tell me!" she said and squeezed past Matt and Pamela to take a seat beside him.

"Well, according to Archimedes, the weight of a person in water seems to be zero. That's because the person displaces an amount of water equal to his or her weight."

Elise scowled. "That's not gossip. That's science!"

"It's all a matter of how you look at it," Ben answered. "I think everyone would be interested to learn how someone like myself can go from one hundred and fifty pounds to zero weight in a matter of minutes."

"Aaaarrrugh . . . You are the most infuriating person I've ever met," exclaimed Elise, poking him playfully in the ribs.

"But you love me just the same, right?" He reached out to grab her arm and pulled her closer.

"Okay, you guys." Jonathan stood up to take charge of the meeting. "You can carry on all you want later. Right now I need to hear ideas on what sort of gala we should throw for the seniors. We want it to be really special."

Dee was the first one to speak up. "Remember the barn dance we all went to at the club in Maryville?" she asked. "Everyone had a great time, so why don't we throw one for the seniors in the gym?"

"A barn dance?" Karen exclaimed, almost choking on her soda.

"Sure," Dee continued. "Why not? It would be fun."

"I don't know." Scott was also doubtful. "Isn't it too close to the proms to have a dance?"

Dee looked at him and frowned. "You've got a point," she admitted. "After the proms everyone will probably be danced out." She shrugged to show there were no hard feelings. "Anyone else have an idea?"

Elise gave her yogurt a stir. "Since we don't want a dance, how about a beach party along the Chesapeake? If we get permission, we could probably have a bonfire."

"What do we do if it rains?" Ben asked with a smile.

Elise turned to him and scowled. "Leave it to you to forecast gloom and doom. It won't rain."

"But what if it does?" he persisted. "We'd have to cancel the whole thing."

"Haven't you ever heard of a tent?" she tried, then realized the ridiculousness of such a suggestion. Even if they did manage to find one that was constructed to stay up in sand, who ever heard of a beach party under a tent?

Everyone agreed a beach party was too chancy, and after a few moments there was silence.

Emily was quietly doodling and suddenly, she lifted her pencil from the napkin and broke into a wide grin. That's it. . . . SENIOR NIGHT! She wrote the two words in big block letters across her napkin. Why didn't I think of it sooner?

She quickly glanced up and found Scott staring at her curiously. "Aren't you going to tell the rest of us?" he asked softly.

Emily met his gaze, then turned to look back down at her napkin. Senior Night had been a tradition at Middlecroft, but could it work at a school as large as Kennedy? Suddenly she wasn't sure. For one thing, it would probably take months to organize, and they had little more than five weeks until graduation. On the other hand, there were lots more people to help, and she remembered hearing how quickly the juniors had put together the Rollerthon last December.

She decided to toss out the idea, and let everyone else decide whether or not it was too big an undertaking.

"I just thought of something," she began. "Only

I'm not sure it's possible." All eyes turned on her, eagerly. "It's an event that was a tradition at Middlecroft, where I used to go to school."

"Will you get to the point already?" Elise chided playfully. "The suspense is killing me."

"Okay, okay. Every spring the junior class at Middlecroft throws a combination carnival and party for the seniors. It's sort of a last blast before graduation."

"Hey, I think that sounds terrific," Jonathan's voice rang out. "It's different, and the seniors should love having a carnival thrown in their honor."

"Especially if we lowly juniors do all the work," Jeremy quipped.

"And lowlier sophomores," Fiona added quickly. "There's no way you're going to leave me out of this."

"Fat chance of that happening when your boyfriend is student activities director," Jeremy said with a laugh.

"We can set up game booths in the gym, and turn the cafeteria into a banquet hall," Emily continued. "Think it will work?"

"I don't see why not." Scott smiled. He was sitting with his elbow on the table and his chin in his hand, staring at her. Emily turned to meet his gaze, and his eyes fixed on her, making everyone else in the room recede into the background. She shivered involuntarily and felt herself blush.

"All right, you guys. I'm all for having a carnival," Jonathan spoke up again. "How about the rest of you?"

Everyone nodded enthusiastically.

"Great idea!" Diana said.

"Yeah, it sure beats a beach party," Ben commented and was rewarded with a playful punch from Elise.

"Okay, then," Jonathan continued. "Now that we've agreed on *what* to do, how about a meeting again tonight to decide *how and when* we're going to do it? We've got a lot of work ahead of us and not much time."

"We can use my house," Elise offered. "I'm sure my parents won't mind."

"Everyone hear that?" Jonathan asked. "Elise's house at eight-thirty?"

There were a few nods, and people started getting to their feet. Fiona and Dee came up to Emily to tell her what a great idea they thought the carnival was. A moment later Elise joined them. Ben had left to speak with his science teacher about his current project, so she suggested they go over to the lunchroom.

"Not me!" Dee said and backed off. "Being around all that food is too much of a temptation — even if most of it *is* lousy!"

In the past year Dee had lost over thirty pounds, and she was determined to keep the weight off.

"Count me out, too." Fiona pushed a lock of blonde hair out of her eyes. "I promised Katie Crawford I'd watch her practice floor exercises. She's working on a new routine and wants my advice on her ballet moves."

"Mention the meeting tonight, in case she wants to come," Elise said.

"Will do," Fiona answered, already moving toward the door.

"How about you?" Elise turned to Emily. "Want to stop off in the lunchroom?"

Emily glanced over her shoulder and saw Scott talking with Marc Harrison and Jonathan. He had hoisted himself on to the edge of the table and sat with his legs dangling, while the other two boys stood before him. Judging by the way Marc was gesturing, Emily figured they were discussing baseball. Last Saturday, Kennedy High had come from behind to win a doubleheader over their arch-rival, Leesburg Academy. No doubt they were replaying those last few moments of the game.

She watched them for another moment, hoping Scott would look at her. Emily considered waiting for him, but then she remembered Heather. She figured Scott was finished talking to her now that the meeting was over.

Emily turned back to Elise. "Sure, I'll come with you." She smiled to hide her disappointment. "We've still got a few minutes left before next period." She gathered up her books, and on her way out the door tossed the uneaten half of her sandwich into the garbage.

Due to a lengthy spring shower, the lunchroom was crowded and noisy. So when she and Elise walked in, they stood by the entrance scanning the crowd until they spotted Woody gesturing for them to join him at his table.

Emily followed Elise past an especially boisterous group of freshmen to where Woody was sitting with other members of the senior crowd.

His girl friend, Kim Barrie, was deep in conversation with Chris Austin, president of the student council. Phoebe Hall, Chris's best friend, was sitting next to her with her head bent over a bowl of hot soup, and Sasha Jenkins, the editor of *The Red and the Gold,* was busy scribbling notes on a yellow legal pad.

"Welcome, fair maidens," Woody said getting up from his chair to give them a sweeping bow. "We were wondering when you'd show up. Do you bring us news of the junior meeting?"

The moment he mentioned the word meeting, all conversation at the table stopped, and a dozen heads turned in their direction. Even Ted, the quarterback for the football team, and Bart Einerson, a linebacker for the team, who was also Diana's older brother, stopped their arm-wrestling.

"What do you want to know?" Elise asked as she reached over to lift a french fry off Kim's plate. "Hope you don't mind," she said, before popping it into her mouth.

"Take us out of our suspense and tell us what you discussed," Woody said dramatically as he pulled out two chairs for them to sit on.

Emily spoke up quickly. "Nothing earth-shattering. Just some problems we were having with the junior prom." She shot her friend a look of warning.

Emily didn't think they should say anything about the carnival until Jonathan got approval from Mr. Barker.

Elise followed with a reticent smile. "There was a little mix-up with the seating arrangements.

It seems a few of the couples were penciled in at more than one table, and it threw the total off by eight."

"Speaking of the prom. . . ." Sasha glanced up from her pad. "Did you hear Peter Lacey just announced the junior and senior queens over WKND?" she paused. "I guess not," she laughed when Emily and Elise looked at her wide-eyed. "Diana Einerson was voted junior prom queen, as expected. But the senior queen must have come as a surprise to some people."

"Who won?" Emily asked.

"Believe it or not, Laurie Bennington!" It was Phoebe who answered this time.

Emily knew who Laurie was from her *Candy Hearts Hotline*, a write-in radio show that offered advice to the lovelorn. Laurie started it soon after Emily came to Kennedy, as a pre-Valentine's Day special.

"I admit she's a bit of a gossip, but she's also gorgeous," Emily said.

"You'll get no argument from me on that last statement," Bart chuckled. "I voted for her."

"Me, too," said Chris, flicking back a lock of golden hair. "As far as I'm concerned, once Brenda took her name off the list of nominees, it was no contest."

Most of the others looked at her as if she'd suddenly gone crazy. A few months ago Chris had been ready to murder Laurie for embarrassing her and Greg over the school radio. In the past, Laurie had also pulled some pretty underhanded tricks on Chris's stepsister, Brenda.

A slow smile spread across Woody's face. "If

28

this is confession time, you can add my name to the list. Laurie's really become a different person. Look at how little campaigning she did for prom queen. She wouldn't even let Dick campaign for her. It was almost as if she didn't expect to win."

"Anyway, she'll make a beautiful prom queen," Sasha said.

"No more beautiful than you would," Kim glanced at her sideways. It was no secret that Sasha had refused to allow her name to be entered for prom queen. Like Brenda, she was a pragmatist and didn't want to get involved in what ultimately came down to a popularity contest.

"Come on, Kim. Don't start that again," Sasha warned. It had been Kim who wanted to put her name up for nomination. "It's all over now, anyway, and I've got to finish this article. It's an interview with Tommy Derringer, the man responsible for our spectacular baseball win over Leesburg."

The mention of the baseball game brought Emily's thoughts back to Scott. She wondered if he was still in the student activities room with Jonathan and Marc, or if he had made his way into the lunchroom unseen, and was now sitting at one of the tables with Heather.

Scott sat in the student activities room only half-listening to Marc and Jonathan discussing the Leesburg game. His mind was on Emily Stevens. When he saw her get up to leave the room, his first impulse was to rush over and ask where she was going. The only reason he'd walked away from her in the first place was because Dee

29

and Fiona had come over, and he didn't want to appear to be eavesdropping on their conversation. But by the time he slid off the table, she was already out the door. She hadn't even turned around to say good-bye.

"You planning to stop off at your locker before next period?" Jonathan asked when he saw Scott get to his feet.

"Huh?" Scott looked at him.

"We're ready to leave, and I asked if you were going to stop by your locker?" Jonathan repeated.

Scott shrugged. "Yeah, I might as well. I don't need my science book any more today." He returned to the table where he'd left his back pack and stood looking at it for a moment before slowly slinging it over his shoulder.

Marc stood watching him impatiently. "Look guys, I'd love to wait around for you, but I promised Dee I'd meet her before my next class. So what do you say I see you later?" He took off out of the room, leaving Scott alone with Jonathan.

"What is it with you today, Phillips?" Jonathan frowned. "We haven't got all day."

"I was thinking about the carnival. Think we'll be able to pull it off?"

"Sure. I'm going to see Mr. Barker again during study period to tell him what we've decided. I don't think he'll object, and provided we're really organized about it. . . ." He looked at Scott quizzically. "That reminds me, how come you decided to show up at the meeting today? You hardly ever come to any of the others."

It was true. Scott wasn't one of your typical

gung-ho Kennedy students, involved in every school project. He chose which ones he wanted to work on, and even then preferred to remain in the background.

There was silence for a moment as they started down the hall. Scott wasn't sure how to answer Jonathan's question without revealing his interest in Emily. She was the real reason he had decided to come to the meeting. There was something about her that interested him.

"Would you believe curiosity?"

"No."

"I see. How about boredom?"

"Not really."

"Okay, I came to the meeting because of a girl." It was the truth, but he knew Jonathan would never believe that now.

"Since when have you ever chased after a girl? And anyway, haven't I seen you riding around with Heather Richardson lately?"

Scott didn't want to take the time to explain his relationship with Heather. He wanted to learn more about Emily.

"Can I ask you a serious question?" He turned to Jonathan, deciding it was worth the risk.

"Sure, go ahead."

They had reached their lockers, and Scott spoke while dialing his combination. "What do you know about Emily Stevens?"

"Let me see." Jonathan still thought Scott was teasing him. "She's cute and bright, and if I wasn't in love with Fiona, I would definitely be interested in her."

Chapter
4

As Emily arrived at Elise's house, she saw Heather's BMW pull up to the curb just in front of her, and her heart began to pound furiously. It was already dark outside, but the light from the front porch gave off enough of a glow for her to make out Scott sitting in the passenger seat. He turned to look at Heather, and Emily felt her jaw tense and her fingernails dig into the palms of each hand. She couldn't help herself. She was jealous.

Had Scott invited Heather to the meeting? For one awful moment Emily feared the answer was yes, and she held her breath. She stood, fists clenched, watching the two figures inside the car. When only one door opened, she gave a heartfelt sigh of relief. A moment later Scott unfolded himself from the car and spotted Emily standing in the driveway.

"Perfect timing," he smiled. "Glad I got a lift."

Emily couldn't keep herself from returning his bright smile. Especially when, after closing the car door, he walked over to her and stared down at her face with a look in his blue-gray eyes that made her feel flushed and breathless.

She didn't even realize Heather had driven away until Scott started for the house. "Might as well head inside."

Emily watched him go, but made no move to follow him.

"Aren't you coming?" Scott asked when he realized she wasn't behind him.

She stood in the driveway, her arms hanging limply at her sides. "I guess," she finally managed, and willed her feet to move.

Elise met them at the door. "Hi, guys. Go on down to the basement. Almost everybody's here already."

As they stepped inside the house, they could hear the din of voices coming from downstairs.

"Sounds like you're having a party." Scott gave her a surprised look.

"I know." Elise giggled. "This thing has really mushroomed since this afternoon. Once everyone heard about Emily's great idea, they all wanted to help. What started out as a small planning meeting has developed into a major planning commission. Katie cut her workout short so she and Eric could be here. Then Karen called and asked if it was all right to bring Brian, even though he missed this afternoon's meeting. Of course I couldn't say no to anybody."

"Of course." Emily laughed.

"I better get a move on," Elise said, pushing up

the sleeves of her sweatshirt, and glancing over her shoulder. "Ben is in the kitchen getting together some munchies, and I've got to go help him. You know the way." She turned away.

Emily led Scott to the basement where the crowd was gathered. Dee and Marc were seated together on the piano bench, playing chopsticks, while Brian, standing beside them with Karen, held his hands over his ears.

"Do you believe the sound coming out of that piano?" he complained to Emily when she and Scott came over.

Emily smiled. "I've heard worse."

"Impossible!"

"You haven't heard Elise play," she teased.

"That bad?"

"Yep!" She began to giggle when she saw her friend come down the stairs carrying an enormous tray filled with cold cuts and cheese. Behind her was Ben with two bowls of pretzels and potato chips.

As soon as Scott saw all the food, he bent over to whisper into Emily's ear. "Is that what she calls 'a few' munchies?"

At that moment Emily wasn't sure what Elise had called them. Scott was standing so close to her she could hardly breathe, much less think clearly.

She watched Elise arrange the food on a table in the corner of the room while Ben set out paper cups for drinks.

"Come on, let's get something to eat before the rest of the vultures get to it." Scott grabbed hold of her arm and dragged her toward the table.

Everyone in the room had the same idea and as the crowd rushed the table, Jonathan said, "C'mon, there'll be plenty of time for you to stuff your faces later. Let's get down to business first. I've still got studying to do later tonight."

Emily settled down on a hassock next to the television. She was joined by Scott, who sat on the thick carpet, his back propped up against the wall.

"First, I want to announce that I spoke to Mr. Barker this afternoon, and he approved our idea for the carnival," Jonathan said once the others had settled down. "We can use the gym and the cafeteria *providing* we agree to clean them up afterward."

Everyone groaned loudly.

"Maybe we can get the freshmen to clean up," Marc suggested from his seat on the piano bench, and the groans turned to cheers.

"Let's wait and see what kind of a mess we're talking about first. We might need the entire school to help us clean up."

Marc laughed. "That would be something."

"You think so? Then you can head up the clean-up committee."

"No way!" Marc shook his head. "I'd rather help set up than clean up!"

"You got it!" Jonathan pointed a finger at him and smiled. "Now before we assign any more job responsibilities," he turned to the others, "I think we'd better let our carnival adviser tell us more about what we've gotten ourselves into."

Emily pushed back a strand of dark hair and smiled. She was sitting cross-legged on the hassock, her paper cup, now empty, resting on one denim-clad knee. "Well, there are really a lot of things to consider." She lifted the empty cup and uncrossed her legs. "We have to decide on the kinds of game booths we want, how many we're going to have, and what prizes to give out. We'll also need to decide how we want the game booths set up. I mean, all water games should be next to one another so we don't mess up the whole gym. Then we need some people to work on publicity and decorations for the gym and cafeteria."

Suddenly everyone started talking at once. "Let's have a baseball throw."

"A ring toss."

"We can decorate the gym with balloons and streamers."

"How about a park theme for the cafeteria?"

Scott whistled for them to be quiet. Then he turned to Emily and smiled. "Go on, they're listening now."

She nodded gratefully before continuing. "At Middlecroft we used to ask the local storekeepers to donate prizes for the game booths. Nothing expensive, just things like a box of stationery, a scarf, or a small stuffed animal. As for food, why don't we ask the seniors' parents to help us. We'll do all the decorating, if they prepare and serve the food."

"Great idea!" Fiona clapped her hands. "I bet Mrs. Barrie would be willing to help." She was Kim's mother and ran Earthly Delights, a very successful catering business.

"Could you ask her?" Emily asked Fiona.

"I'll be glad to speak to the store owners about donating prizes, if you want," said Elise.

"Sure," Ben deadpanned. "Any excuse to go shopping."

For a moment Elise looked defensive. Then she saw Ben smile and flung her arms around his waist. "Right, partner. But I do know most of the store owners in town."

Jonathan, who had been taking all this down on his notepad, glanced up at Emily. "Anything else you want to say?"

She shook her head no and turned the meeting back over to him.

"Okay," he said. "So far I've got Marc taking care of set up, Fiona in charge of food, and Elise and Ben will be responsible for getting the prizes."

"Hey! Wait a minute!" Ben said. "I didn't volunteer for anything."

"I know." Jonathan smiled at him. "That's why I'm appointing you to help Elise." He turned to face the crowd. "Now how about if we hold the carnival the Saturday of Memorial Day weekend. Does that sound okay?"

Everyone agreed and after more discussion, and a short food break, they decided on twelve game booths, with the juniors taking turns working them during the evening. In addition, Karen and Brian said they would announce the carnival on their radio shows, and Dee and Pam both offered to supervise the decorations and design posters. Soon, only the floor plan was left to be worked out.

Jonathan turned to Scott. "Since you've been in charge of designing sets for the school plays, why don't you help Emily work out a floor plan we can show Mr. Barker? And that way we'll know if we have enough room for all the booths."

Scott turned to look at Emily, and his eyes told her he'd be more than willing to help. She smiled, hoping the glow was because he was glad they'd be working closely together, and not because he'd been given an easy job.

When the meeting broke up around ten o'clock, Emily was one of the last ones out the door.

"Need a ride home?" Matt asked. The temperature had dropped and there was a chill in the air.

"No, thanks," Emily said. "I don't mind walking."

"You're sure?" repeated Matt. "It's no trouble. I have to drive Pam home, and we'll be going right past your house."

"Positive," Emily said with a nod, and began buttoning up her sweater. "It's a nice night, and I could use the exercise."

"I'll walk with you," Scott said, coming over to stand beside her.

"That's okay. I only live a couple of blocks from here. I don't mind walking alone."

"Don't you want company?"

"Well, all right." Emily shrugged. She was caught off guard by Scott's offer. Where was Heather? Wasn't she coming to pick him up? She glanced around expecting to see the BMW, but there was no sign of it anywhere.

A gentle breeze came up as they headed down the driveway, blowing Emily's dark hair into her face.

"You cold?" Scott asked when he saw Emily cross her arms snugly.

"Not really." She shivered.

"Liar." He flung open his brown leather jacket and gathered her inside the fold.

Emily gasped as Scott pulled her against him under his jacket. Suddenly they were so close, she could feel his breath against her cheek. It made her shiver again.

"You really are cold," he said when he felt her tremble, and she didn't dare tell him this time she was shivering from his nearness, not because she was cold.

"Try this," he suggested and quickly shrugged out of his jacket to drape it around her shoulders. "I don't really need it."

She started to protest, but Scott just turned her to face him and began zipping the jacket closed.

"Wait, my arms." Emily squirmed, trying to get them into the sleeves. When she succeeded, she felt even more ridiculous. The sleeves of Scott's jacket were so long her fingertips barely showed. Scott lifted a sleeve and peeked in. "Hello in there, anyone home?" he joked.

Emily swatted at him playfully.

"C'mon, I'll guide you." He wrapped a protective arm around her shoulder and began leading her down the sidewalk.

Emily's head came up to the bottom of Scott's chin, and for just a moment she found herself longing to rest it against his shoulder. But the moment passed as they neared the corner.

"We turn left here." She looked at Scott. "I live at the top of the hill."

"The white Victorian house," he said. It wasn't a question.

"How did you know?" Her eyes widened with surprise.

Scott smiled. "My father's an architect. He designed the house across the street from you."

"The English Tudor?"

"That's the one." It was a large two-story house, built with wood and rough stone, and it had enormous windows that overlooked much of Rose Hill.

She hadn't known his father was an architect. In fact she knew little about Scott, other than that he was gorgeous, liked to jog, and belonged to Heather Richardson.

Emily folded her arms more tightly. "Does your father design other things besides houses?" she asked suddenly, in an attempt to rid her mind of Heather.

"Sure. He's done office buildings, hotels, and he just started designing a new wing for an art museum in D.C. I'm going to help him with it this summer." Scott's eyes locked on hers.

"You want to be an architect?"

Scott nodded.

"Since when?"

"I don't know," he shrugged. "All my life, I guess. When I was little, I used to watch my father work at the drawing board. I loved seeing him turn a blank piece of paper into a towering office building or an elegant hotel." He paused to look at her again. "I was even more fascinated when he took me to see the finished product. Imagine creating something sixty-four stories tall."

Emily couldn't help smiling. "It does sound exciting."

Scott pulled her a little closer to his side. "Even designing something as small as the *Oklahoma!* set was exciting," he told her, referring to the musical Kennedy High had put on last fall.

"And the carnival floor plan. . . ?" she asked, remembering the warm look in his eyes earlier.

Emily sensed a sudden change in him. When he spoke again, his voice was different. It was more serious. "Especially the carnival."

The way he said it sent a tiny little shiver racing up and down her spine that didn't go away until they reached her house. They stood awkwardly for a moment on the path leading up to the front door.

"Thanks for walking me home," Emily said, tilting her head back to look at a sky full of thousands of tiny, twinkling stars.

Scott dropped his arm from around her shoulder and turned to face her. "Let me help you get out of my jacket."

Emily stood still as he bent over to unzip it and slide it off her shoulders. "Thanks for letting me wear it," she said as he pulled it over his arms.

He adjusted the collar so it brushed against the hair on the back of his neck, before slipping his hands into the pockets. "You're welcome." He started to turn away, then stopped. "I'm going to take measurements of the gym tomorrow," he added after a moment of silence.

"Okay."

"Then I can start on the floor plan."

"Sounds good."

"I'll need your help deciding where everything should go."

"No problem."

"Okay, see you."

Emily watched Scott disappear back down the hill, feeling as if at any moment her feet might leave the ground, and she would go floating over the rooftops of Rose Hill. She felt light and airy as she savored the memory of walking home with Scott beside her, his arm around her shoulder, and his jacket shielding her from the cold.

Chapter
5

Fiona scribbled a note to Emily on a piece of notebook paper and slipped it to her during study hall. Mr. Baylor was busy correcting history papers and had his head bent over the desk, otherwise she might not have risked it. Old eagle-eyes was quick to spot when a student was goofing off instead of studying, and everyone knew from experience not to incur his wrath.

She watched as Emily unfolded the paper to read the message: *Must talk with you after study hall.* Urgent. *Need advice.* The word 'Urgent' was underlined. Fiona hadn't signed the note, just in case Mr. Baylor intercepted it, but she knew Emily would recognize her fancy script.

Fiona bit her lip. Just before first period she had been summoned into the vice–principal's office and told that her ballet school had just called. They sometimes did that if there was a last minute schedule change, but Fiona didn't have any ballet classes on Friday afternoon.

As she went into Mrs. Goodwin's office to return their call, all sorts of thoughts crowded into her mind. Maybe they'd decided to promote her to another class, or wanted her to audition for a new production. The last thing she expected was to be offered the lead in the ballet school's production of *Coppelia.*

The director of the school explained to her that the girl who was supposed to dance the part of Swanilda had injured her ankle during rehearsal the day before. The ballet was scheduled to open in a week so they needed a replacement immediately. Would she be interested?

Would she! Imagine dancing the lead in *Coppelia.* It didn't matter that it was being performed in high schools throughout the Washington, D.C., area, and not at Kennedy Center. Fiona would be dancing in front of an audience again.

They gave her until Monday to let them know, realizing she would have to get her parents' permission, and Fiona had practically floated into homeroom. It wasn't until she met Dee in the hall on her way to study hall that Fiona's bubble burst. Dee had asked her what she was wearing to the prom.

If she danced in *Coppelia,* she wouldn't be able to *go* to the prom. Would Jonathan understand? He had worked so hard these past few months as chairman of the junior prom committee.

Emily noticed the word urgent was underlined and frowned. She couldn't imagine what the note

44

had to do with. Lots of kids sent her notes asking for love advice, but as far as she knew Fiona and Jonathan weren't having any unusual romantic problems. Had things changed, or did the note have something to do with the carnival?

Emily began chewing on the eraser of her pencil. It was entirely possible, but was that really urgent? She checked her watch and saw there were still another ten minutes left before the bell rang. Whatever urgent meant, it was going to have to wait until then. She folded Fiona's note and slipped it into her jeans pocket. The moment she did she felt the other message she had found in her locker this morning. It was from one of the seniors asking Emily to meet her during lunch today. Apparently someone else needed advice.

People were always slipping notes into Emily's locker. They would slide them in through the slats at the top of her locker door — a sure way to guarantee secrecy. It wasn't because her advice was that much better than the next person's. People turned to Emily because she was willing to listen, and they knew whatever they told her in confidence remained that way.

The moment the bell rang, Emily began gathering up her books.

"Ready, then?" Fiona asked anxiously. In that second Emily knew the "urgent" must be pretty serious. Her friend's blue eyes looked very troubled. And she was nervously pulling at several strands of blonde hair.

"Why don't we go to the little niche behind the stairwell and talk?" Emily suggested in an effort to put Fiona at ease. "No one will crash into us there, and it's a lot quieter than standing in the hallway."

Fiona agreed, and they hurried out of the room. There were only five minutes between classes, which wasn't a lot of time, so the moment they reached the niche, Fiona started talking. "Emily, the most wonderful thing has just happened to me. Only I'm afraid it's going to turn into the most terrible, at least as far as Jonathan is concerned."

"Go on," Emily urged.

"I've been asked to dance the lead in my ballet school's production of *Coppelia*." Fiona's face brightened. "It's being given especially for inner-city kids, and there are eight performances scheduled. Can you imagine how exciting it will be? Most of those children have never seen a live ballet before."

Without waiting for an answer, she continued, "I've always dreamed of starring in this ballet. I just can't say no to it. I've been working toward this ever since I resumed my dancing in the States. But if I agree to dance in *Coppelia*, I won't be able to go to the junior prom with Jonathan." Her large blue eyes beseeched Emily. "I need you to help me," she begged. "I don't know how to tell him."

Emily understood her concern. She remembered Fiona telling her about the arguments she and Jonathan had had when they first started dating. Fiona had been new at Kennedy, and so caught up in her own problems, and anxieties about dancing, she hadn't paid attention to the things that were important to Jonathan — like the Holiday Fund for the Homeless he organized just before Christmas.

"I think you should be honest with him," Emily said thoughtfully.

"And say what?"

"Tell him exactly what you just told me. That this is an opportunity of a lifetime, and you can't pass it up."

Fiona dropped her eyes. "He'll never buy it. You know how Jonathan is when it comes to his school projects. The prom is the most important thing to him right now."

"You won't know until you try."

"What if he doesn't want to listen?"

"Make him listen. Your dancing means a lot to you, too." Emily put a comforting arm around her friend.

Fiona sighed. "Will you come with me?"

"You don't really want me there," she squeezed her shoulder. "You have to do this yourself."

"You're right." She gave Emily a weak smile. "I'll try and tell Jonathan during lunch. And thanks for the advice. I knew I could count on you." Her face brightened a bit, but she still looked worried.

Jonathan was lying on his back in the grass with his head pillowed in his arms when Fiona got to the quad. It was a beautiful day and most of the Kennedy High student body was spending their lunch hour basking in the late spring sunshine.

"Hello," she said, coming to stand over him. He looked so handsome with the top three buttons of his blue Oxford shirt undone, and the sleeves pushed up over his muscled forearms.

"Oh, hi." Jonathan scrambled into a sitting position and pulled her forward for a kiss. "I've been looking for you all morning. Where have you been hiding?"

Fiona slid her book bag off her shoulder and sank to the grass beside him. "In class, where else?" she smiled.

She didn't want to let on she'd been avoiding him until after she had a chance to rehearse what she was going to say. Unfortunately, it wasn't possible for her to dance in *Coppelia* and go to the prom with Jonathan. Because even if she didn't take a curtain call, it would still be after eleven by the time she changed her clothes and dashed across town.

Fiona shifted her legs to a more comfortable position and looked at Jonathan. On the surface she knew she appeared calm and cool, but inside she was a bundle of nerves. She hoped Jonathan would understand.

Just as she leaned forward and opened her mouth to begin, Jonathan glanced over her shoulder. "Hey, Forrest, over here!"

Fiona turned around and saw Elise and Ben with their fingers entwined, heading in their direction. Just behind them were Dee and Marc.

"Hi, guys," Dee said, sinking down onto the grass beside Fiona. "We couldn't find you in the lunchroom. Then Emily told us you were out here with the rest of the sun-worshippers."

Fiona smiled at her weakly. "Uh-huh. It's less noisy out here." She had left a note in the student activities room asking Jonathan to meet her in the quad during lunch. She had hoped they'd have at least a few moments alone so she could tell him about *Coppelia* without everyone else around.

"Hey, are you okay?" Dee touched her shoulder gently. "You look a little pale."

Fiona pasted a smile on her face. "I'm okay. Really. I've just got a lot on my mind right now."

"You're not the only one," Jonathan said, leaning over to wrap his arm around her shoulder. "When I volunteered to be chairman of the prom committee, I really thought all I'd have to do was find a hotel ballroom and hire a band. Boy, was I wrong! There are a million headaches that go along with the job. Like this morning, when a couple, who shall remain anonymous, came up to me and asked to have their table changed. It seems they had a disagreement with one of the other couples at the same table, and now they don't want to sit with them."

"What did you do?" Elise asked as she ran her fingers through Ben's hair. He was lying on the grass with his head in her lap.

"Since it's really too late for *me* to make any changes in the seating arrangements, I got them to agree to find another couple who would be willing to switch seats with them."

"I don't know, Preston." Ben squinted against the brightness of the sky. "You seem to have a way of sweet-talking people into doing things. Look how you managed to get me involved in writing publicity for the Rollerthon."

"You loved every minute of it." Elise tousled his hair playfully.

"Speak for yourself." He pulled a handful of grass and tossed it at her. The whole idea for a fund-raiser to help the Stamp Out Hunger in the U.S. charity had been hers. "I will admit one thing." He laughed when some of the grass landed on Elise's head. "It wasn't as much work as the prom."

"Yeah," Jonathan chuckled. "But unlike you, I enjoy hard work."

"Would you listen to him." Mark rolled his eyes. "A minute ago he was complaining about all the work he has to do as chairman. But now, when we sympathize with him, he turns around and starts telling us he really enjoys it. Make up your mind, Preston, which is it?"

"You want the truth?" Jonathan sat up straighter. "I know I don't have to put in as much work as I do on the prom. But the reason I've been so involved in every detail is because I want this to be the best junior prom in the history of Kennedy High. And it will be." His voice was full of excitement. "We've already sold more tickets than ever before, and the extra money is being used to have a buffet on the hotel terrace before the prom. I'm telling you, it's going to be the ultimate as far as proms go."

He didn't see Fiona's face fall. If she had been nervous about telling Jonathan about her prom conflict before, it was nothing compared to how she felt now.

She leaned her head back and closed her eyes. What was she going to do?

"Working on your tan for the prom?" a playful voice sounded above her, and Fiona opened her eyes to see Laurie Bennington smiling down at her. As usual, she looked like she had just stepped off the front page of a fashion magazine.

"Hey, Laurie, congratulations on being named senior prom queen," Ben called out.

"Thanks," she smiled and ran a hand along the wide neck of her cherry red top. "That's the reason I stopped by. I've decided to throw a big party for Diana and me tomorrow to celebrate our being chosen prom queens. I know it's awfully short notice," she apologized. "But we hope all of you will be able to come, anyway."

"What's this I hear about a party?" Woody said, sauntering up to them with Kim and Sasha by his side.

Laurie pushed her short dark hair away from her face and stepped up to him. "Don't worry, Woody, you're invited. You, too, Sasha and Kim." She smiled.

"Sounds like fun," Sasha said. "Only Rob won't be here this weekend."

Laurie shrugged. "So come without him. You know my parties are never for couples only."

Everyone was buzzing about the party except Fiona, who was no longer paying attention. Instead she was caught up in her own thoughts concerning Jonathan and the prom.

"Well, is everybody free tomorrow?" Laurie asked. "Diana and I really want all of our friends to be there."

"Sounds all right to me," Jonathan smiled and turned to look at Fiona. "How about it?" he asked.

Laurie's parties were always the best. Her

51

house was enormous and she had a huge back-yard, complete with tennis courts and a swimming pool. There was plenty of room for dancing in the living room, and she usually showed the latest videos on the large television screen in the den.

It suddenly occurred to Fiona that the party would be the perfect place to tell Jonathan she wouldn't be going to the prom. He'd be having such a good time he probably wouldn't get angry. It would also give her a whole extra day to plan a new speech.

"Yes," she said. "I'd love to go to the party."

Chapter
6

Fiona woke up with the sun on Saturday morning and lay staring up at the ceiling. Overnight her resolve to tell Jonathan about her conflict had weakened, and she didn't feel ready to face the new day. Maybe if she could fall back asleep for a little while things would take care of themselves.

She rolled onto her stomach and squeezed her eyes tightly shut. Her parents had been thrilled when she told them about her chance to dance in *Coppelia*. Even Jeremy promised to bring Diana to one of her performances. So why was she so afraid to tell Jonathan?

Fiona pulled the covers over her head and breathed deeply. There was no getting around it, she had to tell him tonight. The longer she put it off, the more difficult it would become. If he wasn't going to be understanding, she might as well find that out. And if he was, all the more reason to share the joy with him.

A gentle breeze stirred her curtains and carried with it the lively sound of birds chirping. Fiona slid out of bed into a pool of golden sunlight that streamed in through her open window. It was unusual for her to be up this early on a Saturday, but since she couldn't sleep she might as well get dressed and go downstairs.

"Hey, what are you doing up so early?" Jeremy asked when she entered the kitchen.

"I'm going for a walk," she told him on impulse. It suddenly sounded like a good idea. Fiona knew she'd never have any peace with Jeremy sitting in the kitchen. He was still somewhat overprotective and always trying to shield her from getting hurt.

"Hey! Wait a minute. There's something I want to ask you." He put down his orange juice.

"What?"

"How are you going to break the news to Jonathan?"

"About *Coppelia*?"

Jeremy nodded.

"I'm going to tell him straight out," Fiona told her brother and walked out the door.

As she walked, Fiona paid little attention to where she was going. When she finally did stop and look up, she was rather amazed to find herself at the edge of Rose Hill Park. She hadn't realized she had walked so far. She decided to take a stroll down one of the tree-lined paths. In the distance she could see a lone jogger running in her direction. But the sun was in her eyes, so Fiona couldn't make out who it was until the jogger was almost upon her.

"Emily!" she called out, stunned to see her friend jogging so early. It was only a little after nine. Emily was just as surprised to see Fiona. "What are you doing here?" She came to a halt and looked around as if she expected to see someone else.

Fiona flushed. For a moment she didn't know what to say. "Just taking a walk." She stuck her hands into her pockets.

"How'd it go with Jonathan yesterday? Did you talk to him?"

Again Fiona felt uneasy. "No, not yet." Suddenly she couldn't look Emily in the eye.

There was a long silence while both girls waited for the other to say something. When Emily realized what was happening, she walked over to a nearby bench and sat down. She sensed Fiona needed to talk. "Want to tell me about it?"

Fiona smiled weakly and sat down. "I tried telling him yesterday," she began, leaning forward to rest her chin in her hands. "But before I could get a word out, he started raving about how wonderful the prom was going to be and how hard he had been working to make it the best ever." She shook her head. "After hearing that, I couldn't bring myself to say anything."

Emily squeezed her friend's hand. "Well, that's okay. But you're going to have to tell him sometime."

Fiona sat up and stared straight ahead. She loved Jonathan. He was a big part of her life and during the few months they'd been a couple, they had shared so many things. But remembering the look on his face yesterday, she couldn't help wondering if he would be able to share her joy at being asked to dance the lead in *Coppelia*.

She turned to look at Emily. "Why does the prom have to be next week? Why couldn't it be two weekends from now?"

"Things don't always work out the way you want them to."

"I know and it's not fair!"

"What's not fair is for you to let Jonathan go on thinking you'll be going to the prom," Emily told her gently. "If you love him, you have to trust him enough to believe he'll understand."

Fiona looked up at the sun peeking above the treetops and sighed. She knew Emily was right. She wasn't being fair to Jonathan or herself. "I promise I'll tell him tonight at Laurie's party," she said.

Fiona took her time getting ready for the party. During the course of the day, she found her nervousness increasing and knew if she rushed it would only get worse. She took a long shower, and after shampooing her silky blonde hair, let the warm soapy water cascade over her shoulders and down her back. Then she stood before her closet examining her wardrobe before finally selecting a pair of royal blue stirrup pants and a wide-necked pullover sweater.

She slipped into the clothes and turned to look at her reflection in the full-length mirror on her wall. Something was missing, she decided, and opened her drawer to pull out a blue silk scarf. She looped it around her neck and just as she finished tying it, Jonathan drove up in Big Pink, his old Chevy convertible.

He honked the horn twice, and Fiona went downstairs to meet him at the front door.

"You look terrific," he said when she flung the door open.

"Thank you," Fiona said, following him out to his car. Jeremy had already left to pick up Diana, which meant they would be driving to the party alone.

She slid into the front seat and watched him walk around to the driver's side. He looked so tall and handsome in a navy blue polo shirt and well-tailored chinos. She couldn't see his feet until he lowered his long form into the car. Then she noticed he was wearing a pair of cordovan loafers instead of his usual high-top sneakers.

"Hey, beautiful — smile." Jonathan cupped her face in his hands and kissed her gently on the mouth. Fiona closed her eyes and let his kisses wipe away her fears and nervousness. When the kiss ended, and he continued to hold her, all Fiona let herself think about was how wonderful Jonathan's arms felt around her.

They rode to Laurie's in silence. Fiona stared down at their clasped hands, then over at Jonathan. His warm gray eyes were focused on the road, giving her a chance to study him intently. She remembered the first time she saw Jonathan. It was when he came to pick her up to take her to her very first American football game. Her brother Jeremy had had this wild idea that Fiona needed a boyfriend to help her adjust to living in the United States, and had fixed her and Jonathan up on a blind date. As it turned out, she had hated the football game, but no matter how hard she tried she couldn't hate Jonathan. Instead she had fallen in love with him.

He pulled into the horseshoe driveway and cut the engine. "This sure is some impressive place."

Maybe now was the time to tell him, Fiona thought. But before she had a chance to say anything he was out of the car.

"Aren't you coming?" He peeked in the window.

Fiona slid out the passenger door. "Let's go in through the backyard," she suggested absent-mindedly. "It's easier than walking around the front."

Jonathan gave a short laugh. "Your wish is my command," he said, linking her arm through his.

Fiona tensed, but didn't pull away. "You really mean that?"

"As long as you don't ask me to jump off a bridge or something equally ridiculous."

"Like miss the prom," she asked, hoping to get a reaction from Jonathan that would give her some idea of what to expect when she told him about *Coppelia.*

He threw back his head and laughed. "I don't know about you, but I'd sooner jump off a bridge."

Fiona sensed he wasn't joking and an awful feeling constricted her chest. She had wanted a reaction from Jonathan — and she had gotten one. Now she wished she'd never asked.

Jonathan reached for her hand as he led her through the unlocked gate into the beautifully landscaped backyard. Beyond the patio decorated with hanging lanterns, there was a swimming pool and a Japanese rock garden, complete with a little waterfall.

"Hey, Laurie, I think you've got a couple of gate crashers," Woody called out when he saw them coming around the side of the house.

A moment later Laurie appeared in the terrace doorway, determined to fend off the unexpected guests. When she saw it was only Fiona and Jonathan, she grinned. "It's you!" She came over to give them a hug, looking very dramatic in a red jumpsuit and big red earrings to match. "Your brother was just asking if you were here yet." She took Fiona's free hand. "Come inside so he can stop worrying."

Fiona followed Laurie into the living room where half a dozen couples were dancing to music blasting from the stereo. Jeremy was on the other side of the room, watching the dancers with Diana.

When he saw his sister come in, he waved and came over to her. "Laurie sure knows how to throw a party," he shouted above the music. "Where's Jonathan?"

"Out on the patio talking to Woody and some other people." She smiled thinly.

Diana picked up on her mood immediately. "Hey, you okay?"

"Yeah. I'm fine." Fiona tried to be upbeat. "I just came inside, too, because Laurie said Jeremy was getting a little crazy with brotherly concern."

She gave her brother a playful punch in the arm. "Now, if you don't mind, I'm going to take a look around." What she really wanted to do was disappear. Then she wouldn't have to tell Jonathan she couldn't go to the prom with him.

She put her fists in her pockets to hide her apprehension, and started wandering through the rooms. Now that she had an idea of how Jonathan was going to react to her news, she needed to work up the courage to tell him. She already knew what she was going to say. In fact she practically had her little speech memorized. All that was left was getting Jonathan away from the crowd because she didn't want him making a scene.

She wandered into the library and sat herself down on the soft leather couch. It was quiet in there, and dark, except for a single lit lamp on the large mahogany desk opposite the fireplace. Fiona leaned her head back against the chocolate-brown cushions and stared at the rows of books lined up neatly on the wooden shelves against the wall. She had a feeling if she were to check closely, she'd find them arranged alphabetically by author.

"Here you are," Jonathan said as he walked into the library a few moments later, carrying a slice of pizza. "Want a bite?" He held it up to her.

She shook her head. "No thanks."

"No? What is it, Fiona? Something's wrong."

This was it. She knew she couldn't put it off any longer. She had to tell him now.

She returned his gaze without blinking. "I've

been asked to dance the lead in *Coppelia*," she said in a controlled, even voice. "It's something I've dreamed of ever since I started dancing, and I just can't turn it down. But there's a problem." She paused, trying to keep her voice under control. "It means I won't be able to go to the prom."

She watched Jonathan's face slowly register his disbelief. "I don't get it. Is this some kind of joke?"

Fiona shook her head.

"I can't believe it. When did you find out?" he asked, setting aside his half-eaten slice of pizza.

Fiona wrapped her arms around her chest. "They called me at school yesterday morning."

"You knew about this yesterday and didn't tell me?"

Fiona winced, recalling how she had sat in the quad listening to everyone discuss the prom, and never once said a word. "I wanted to tell you," she said weakly. "But I was scared."

"Scared?" Jonathan looked at her with a combination of pain and anger on his face. "Of what? That I might get crazy?" He jammed his fists into his pockets and fell back against the closed door.

"Something like that," Fiona said softly.

Jonathan shook his head. "I don't believe you're doing this to me." He pushed himself away from the wall. "You know how much I've been looking forward to going to the prom. It's one of the most important events of the school year, and just about everybody is going to be there."

"Jonathan, you don't understand."

"Oh, yes I do. All you care about is your ballet. In fact you're so caught up with dancing, you never even stop to think what's important to the rest of us — or consider how we feel."

"That's not true!"

"It sure is," he snapped. "And the crazy thing is, I have no one to blame but myself. *I* was the one who made you audition for the Academy of Ballet Arts, anyway."

Fiona stood up from the couch. "Go ahead and blame yourself if it will make you feel better," she said angrily. "I knew you wouldn't understand. That's why I waited so long to tell you."

Jonathan's eyes suddenly clouded with pain. "Ever since we met I've supported you, and what do I get in return? Zip." He shook his head sadly. "This is one of the most important nights of my life, and my girl friend is going to be off dancing in a ballet. It's pretty obvious where your priorities stand."

"Oh, Jonathan." Fiona's anger disappeared the moment she saw the hurt in his eyes. "I want to be with you, but I can't pass up this opportunity. This will be one of the important nights of *my* life, too."

"Sure." He laughed harshly. "I'm tired of this. It's time you tried to understand how I feel for a change." He looked at her for a final moment, then spun around on his heels. "You can get Jeremy to drive you home."

"Please don't go," Fiona begged when he walked toward the door. Tears were already flowing freely down her cheeks.

He turned back to her, and shook his head slowly. "I'm sorry, Fiona. I'm really going to miss you, but I don't think we should see each other anymore."

Then he disappeared down the hall, and Fiona's heart sank.

Chapter
7

Emily walked out onto the red brick patio. The air was fresh and deliciously cool, so for a few minutes she just stood there, looking out at the backyard bathed in a soft silvery glow from the half moon. One brilliant star low in the horizon was visible through a cluster of trees behind the swimming pool, and she could make out a little waterfall cascading down the rock garden and splashing into a small pond at the bottom.

She went to sit on the step at the edge of the patio as the melodic sound of water rippling down the rocks filled the backyard. Everything else was quiet, muted. No birds sang, and the music coming from inside the house was muffled.

She lifted her head to gaze up at the sky, and spotted a lone figure silhouetted in the light from the doorway. She knew immediately it was Scott. His long legs, wide shoulders, and casual stance were all familiar to her. And as he walked over to her, she wondered how long he had been standing there.

"Is this step reserved, or can anybody sit here?" he asked, looking down at her.

"Help yourself."

"Will do." Scott sat down on the step.

Emily quickly shifted her position to put more space between them. She didn't want their shoulders touching. "What brings you out here?" she asked after a short silence.

Scott leaned over to rest his forearms on his knees. "Getting some air. How about you?"

"I'm listening to the waterfall."

"Makes you want to kick off your shoes and stick your toes under the icy water, doesn't it?" Scott smiled.

Emily nodded.

"Let's do it!"

The suggestion was totally unexpected, and for a moment Emily didn't respond.

"You and me?" she finally asked, her blue eyes searching his face.

"You see anyone else out here?" He put his hand on the small of her back and gave her a gentle nudge.

Emily held back. More than anything she wanted to walk to the waterfall with Scott. But at the same time she knew it would be wrong. She couldn't put Heather out of her mind.

"Well?" Scott asked softly. "Do you want to?"

Emily turned to him, about to refuse. But before she had a chance to say no, Bart and Holly stepped onto the patio.

"Hey, Phillips," Bart teased, when he saw Scott sitting on the step with her. "Where's your chauffeur tonight?" It was obvious he was referring to Heather.

"Her grandmother's visiting for the weekend, so she had to take part of the night off," Scott shot back.

"Too bad. Let me know if you need a lift home."

"Thanks. Will do," Scott answered, and turned back to Emily as Bart and Holly drifted over to the far end of the patio.

Emily drew her knees under her and leaned forward, confused. There was something very odd about Scott's reaction to Bart's teasing. He seemed to be treating it as a joke, yet he didn't strike her as the type of guy who would make fun of his girl friend.

"Ready?" Scott stood up, and stuck out his hand to help Emily to her feet. She sat up straight and quickly shrugged off her concern. Suddenly all she cared about was the fact that Heather wasn't at the party.

"I guess," she said, and instinctively reached out to take his hand.

The moment their fingers touched Emily felt a warm current flow through her body. She couldn't move. For just a second all she could do was sit there and stare up at him. Scott had his back to the lanterns strung around the edges of the patio, but she was still able to see his features. She didn't think he had ever looked more handsome. His blue-gray eyes were staring down at her with a soft look, and his slightly disheveled blond hair was awash in moonlight. When he smiled, Emily thought she might melt.

As they made their way across the lawn, a light spring breeze rustled the tree branches, blowing tendrils of hair across Emily's face. When it became still again, she tossed her head back to shake the hair away, and noticed the bright star she had spotted earlier was now surrounded by thousands of others, all twinkling overhead.

She turned to say something to Scott and noticed him staring at her intently. They were no longer holding hands, yet there was something about his gaze that gave her a warm feeling. It was the same every time they were alone together. All Scott had to do was look at her, and she felt herself start to tingle.

When they reached the waterfall, she stood there in silent wonder. It was only four feet high, but the waterfall, flooded with soft light, looked beautiful as the water cascaded down the rocks. Emily looked to see where the light was coming from and noticed tiny spotlights among the rocks and ferns that rimmed the pond.

"It's really lovely," she sighed.

"My father's firm designed it for the Benningtons last summer," Scott informed her softly. "They don't usually do landscape architecture, but it was too much of a challenge to refuse. They also designed that humpback bridge over there."

Emily followed his gaze and saw a tiny arched bridge at the edge of the pond opposite the waterfall.

"Can you walk across it?" she asked. From where she stood it didn't look very sturdy.

"Of course. Go give it a try."

Emily crossed the bridge and found herself on a tiny island. In the center was a white wrought-iron bench, and her eyes lit up at the unexpected sight. It was all too perfect. The moonlight, the waterfall, and the little humpback bridge reaching over to the tiny island. "I feel like I've just stepped into a fairyland, and any minute a prince will come by on a white horse and carry me away," she said.

"Hang on, I'm coming," Scott called. He raced across the bridge and scooped her up in his arms.

Suddenly his face was so close, she felt like she was spinning. Scott's features blurred, and all Emily could feel was his sweet breath against her cheek. When he started carrying her across the bridge, her heart thumped wildly.

It was Scott who broke the spell a moment later when a bullfrog jumped out of the pond and landed by his feet. He looked down at the frog. "Do you think he's a prince in disguise?"

Emily followed his gaze. "I'm not going to kiss him to find out."

Scott laughed and set her on her feet. Then he walked over to the waterfall and crouched down to watch the water cascade over the rocks.

Emily straightened her lime-green sweater and followed. "Where is the water coming from?" she asked in an effort to appear calm. "I don't see any stream."

Scott looked up at her and smiled. "That's because it's a manmade waterfall. The pond is fed by underground springs, and the water is pumped up onto the rocks."

"It must be very cold, then."

"Depends on what you consider cold." Scott smiled mischievously, and sitting back on the grass, started pulling off his sneakers and socks.

As Emily watched him, she began having doubts. "Are you sure it's okay to do this? I mean, I don't want us to get into trouble or anything."

"Aw, come on," Scott gave her an innocent smile. "How can we get into trouble? All we're going to do is stick our feet under the waterfall. We aren't going to hurt anything."

She still made no move to take off her shoes.

"Don't tell me you're going to chicken out?" Scott teased.

"Who, me?"

"Yes, you."

"No way!" Emily started pulling off her shoes.

"That's what I like, a girl who's willing to live dangerously." He bent over to roll up his pants.

Emily did the same before joining him on the rocks rimming the pond.

"Ladies first," Scott urged once she had sat down beside him.

Emily shook her head. "Oh, no. You go first."

"How about if we do it together?"

"Okay."

They stuck their feet out and let the cascading water tumble onto their toes.

"Oh, man. This is great." Emily laughed as the cold water both numbed and tickled her feet.

"Yeah, it is." Scott wiggled his toes. "It reminds me of when I used to have water fights in a stream I used to swim in as a kid." He jumped off the rocks into the pond. "I was pretty good at it, too." Without warning, he scooped up a handful of water and tossed it at Emily.

She stiffened from the shock as it sprayed all over her. "I'll get you for that!" She slid into the pond.

"You think so?" Scott laughed.

"Just watch me." She bent over to scoop up some water. But he was too fast for her. In one swift movement he had jumped out of the pond, scooped up his sneakers, and started running full speed toward the house.

"You don't play fair," Emily told him when she reached the patio and found him seated on the step.

Scott looked at her and laughed. "Who said anything about fair? I just mentioned I was good at water fights."

Emily sank down onto the step and began rolling down her pants. "Look at me, I'm soaked!"

"I'm looking." He stared right into her eyes. "And it looks good to me."

Emily felt a sudden flush, as if the temperature had just shot up to ninety-five. With those few words Scott had sent her heart racing so fast she thought for sure he could hear the thumping noise. She busied herself wiping off her feet, but when she looked up again after putting on her shoes, he was still staring at her.

"How about some pizza?" he suggested softly.

Emily hesitated. "I. . . ."

"Laurie ordered it special from Mario's. I saw the delivery van arrive earlier."

"Pizza does sound good."

"Does that mean yes?"

Emily nodded.

"Good," Scott affirmed, his eyes twinkling. "I'm starved, and I hate eating alone."

Chapter
8

Emily picked up her slice of pizza and bit into the thin crust.

"How is it?" Scott asked, scooping up a slice for himself.

"Mmmm, good," Emily mumbled, reaching for a napkin to wipe off the oil that had dripped down between her fingers. No matter how careful she was when eating pizza, she always managed to make a mess.

"You've also got tomato sauce on your face."

"Where?"

"Right over here." Scott gently ran his finger across her cheek.

"I'm not very good at eating pizza," she said, blushing.

"Who is?"

"You don't seem to be having any trouble." They were alone in the kitchen, sitting opposite each other at the white Formica counter, and

Scott was already working on his second slice.

"Just lucky tonight."

Emily reached for a can of soda and took a long sip. "How are you with ice-cream cones? I always wind up licking the ice cream off my arm."

"At least that's better than licking it off your sweater." They both burst out laughing.

Scott was so easy to be with. He knew how to laugh and have a good time, yet there was a serious side to him, too. Emily had seen it when he'd told her he wanted to be an architect, and she sensed it whenever he looked at her with that penetrating gaze — as if he was trying to communicate something to her.

"Watch this." He turned in his seat and aimed the crust of his pizza at a garbage pail across the kitchen. It hit the rim, then bounced in.

"Good shot," Emily applauded. "Want to try it again?" She held out her crumpled napkin.

"Promise not to jeer if I miss?"

"Scout's honor." Emily raised two fingers in the air.

He tossed the napkin toward the garbage pail, but it fell a few inches short. "Can't win 'em all." He shrugged, getting up to cross the kitchen.

Emily watched him scoop the napkin off the floor and in one easy motion toss it over his head. This time it went straight in. "Bull's-eye!"

Scott came back to the counter, but instead of returning to the stool, he stood next to her with one arm leaning on the counter in front of her. "Let's go see what movie they're watching in the den."

Emily was very confused by Scott's behavior.

She loved being with him, and she was having a good time, but how could she let herself get so attached to someone who had a girl friend already? And if he had a girl friend, why was he treating her like this? Word was bound to get back to Heather.

She almost said something to Scott about it, but stopped when she found him looking at her, his face boyish and expectant. For a moment the room was very quiet. Then he reached out and took her hand in his.

"Wait," she exclaimed. "I haven't finished my soda."

"Take it with you," Scott said, leading her into the den where everyone was sprawled out across the floor.

The room was dimly lit, except for the giant screen, and there were bodies everywhere. Emily clutched Scott's hand tightly as he started to weave his way through the crowd, looking for a place to sit. It was difficult to see the floor, and there wasn't a lot of room to maneuver. At one point while tiptoeing around, Emily tripped over an extended leg.

"Sorry," she said when Jeremy looked up. He spotted her holding Scott's hand, and gave her a puzzled look. When Elise noticed them weaving their way past her and Ben, she too looked at them peculiarly.

"There's room for two more over here," Bart called out in a loud whisper.

Emily quickly sat herself down on the floor, and slid low against the wall in order to hide from any more curious glances. Surprisingly, the reactions didn't faze Scott. He settled down easily, and after a moment he leaned toward her, and plucked the soda can from her lap. "May I?" he winked.

"Where have you guys been?" Bart whispered as Scott tilted the can back to take a swallow. "You missed a crucial scene."

"We were in the kitchen eating pizza."

"All this time? Did you leave any for the rest of us?" he joked.

Emily was about to tell him that there were still two pizzas on top of the stove, when she noticed Diana whispering something into Laurie's ear. A moment later Laurie turned around to casually look in their direction.

Scott didn't even seem to notice, or if he did, he didn't seem the least bit concerned. He had his legs stretched out in front of him and his arms crossed casually across his stomach. Between whispered conversations with Bart, or Ted Mason, who was stretched out on the floor next to his girl friend Molly, Scott would turn to Emily with a happy smile on his face. At one point he lifted his arm to rest it on her shoulder, and his touch seemed to echo through her body. She closed her eyes to hide what she was feeling and hoped he didn't notice the pink flush that was coloring her cheeks.

It certainly seemed that Scott was quite interested in her. Could she have been mistaken about his feelings for Heather? A ray of hope began to brighten her spirits, and when Scott began to smooth his fingers over her shoulder, Emily let herself relax.

As soon as the movie was over and Laurie had flicked on the lights, Scott straightened up and got to his feet. Everyone was drifting out of the den and soon music started blasting from the stereo again.

Instead of following the crowd, Scott took Emily's hand and led her into the hall. She was about to ask where they were going when she heard a strange, muffled noise coming from the library. She opened the door and peeked inside. Fiona was sitting by herself on the leather couch, with her head in her hands, sobbing.

Emily turned to Scott. "I'll be right back. I've got to talk to Fiona."

"Why? Is something wrong?"

"I'm not sure. I think she and Jonathan had an argument." Why else would Fiona be crying?

"Okay." Scott looked at her with a combination of understanding and disappointment.

She made her way over to the couch and sat down. When Fiona didn't acknowledge her presence, Emily reached out and touched her arm gently.

Fiona broke away from Emily and walked over to the bay window overlooking the swimming pool. Emily followed her and sat on the window ledge.

"Do you want to tell me what happened?" Emily asked softly. "It might make you feel better to talk about it."

Fiona pressed her forehead against the glass.

"There's nothing to talk about. It's over. Jonathan broke up with me."

"Are you sure?" Emily asked. She couldn't believe they were finished. "I can understand him being disappointed, but he loves you too much to call it quits just because you aren't going to the prom."

Fiona swung around, tears spilling down her cheeks. "Well, he did!" she said, and pressed her lips together. "He said it was over and walked out. It was awful."

Emily watched Fiona cry for a moment, then stood up and put her arms around her friend. "Give him time. He'll come back."

Fiona pulled away. "Oh, Emily, do you think so? If it weren't for Jonathan, I would never have had this opportunity to dance in *Coppelia*. I might not be dancing at all." She wiped her tears with the back of her hand. "I'm okay now. Thanks," she said after a moment.

"You sure?"

"Yes."

"Is there anything I can do?"

"You could let me bum a ride home with you." Fiona gave her a weak smile.

Emily nodded and returned her smile. "I'm really sorry things turned out this way."

Fiona nodded sadly. "Me, too. Maybe if I'd listened to you and told Jonathan right away, he wouldn't have been so hurt."

"Maybe if you try talking to him again. . . ."

Fiona shook her head sadly. "I don't think he'll listen to anything I have to say right now." She lifted her hands to her face.

"Come on." Emily put her arm around Fiona and started leading her toward the door. "We're going home right now."

"Thanks for making me talk about it, Em. You were right, it helped. I just hope I didn't spoil the party for you."

"Don't worry about it."

Just before Emily and Fiona reached the door, it opened, and Elise peeked her head in. "Hope I'm not interrupting," she looked at Fiona. "I just saw Scott and he told me you were in here. Is everything okay?"

"Are you and Ben ready to leave?" asked Emily.

"Sure, if you want. I'll go in and get him. We'll meet you by the car." She darted down the hall.

Emily and Fiona slipped out the kitchen door. The last thing Fiona needed was to face the others. The moment they saw her crying they would insist on knowing what had happened.

As they made their way over to the car, it flashed through Emily's mind that she hadn't said good-night to Scott. She didn't want to leave without seeing him again, and she was about to go back into the house when she noticed someone rushing toward them. As the figure came closer she realized it was Scott, and she felt a rush of excitement flow through her. He skirted around the rear of one car and jumped over the front bumper of another.

"Elise told me you were leaving," he said when he reached her side.

Emily nodded. "I was coming to tell you. I'm taking Fiona home."

Scott reached out for her hand and led her a few feet away from the car. "How about if I call you tomorrow? We can go jogging."

Emily's face lit up. "Okay."

"Is ten o'clock too early?"

"No, that's fine," she said. " 'Bye." She headed back to the car with a lightness in her step.

Chapter
9

When Emily woke up on Sunday and looked out her bedroom window, her heart sank. The sky was dark and gloomy, and she could hear faint rumblings of thunder in the distance. Why today? she mumbled, as another clap of thunder sounded, closer this time.

She slipped out of bed and walked over to the window to get a closer look at the threatening sky. Clouds were building overhead and a strong breeze had picked up, bending the branches of trees lining the Stevens' driveway. A moment later the first large drop fell from the sky, followed by another and another, until the rain was coming down steadily.

Emily flung herself onto her bed and buried her face in the pillow. It was feathery soft and wrapped around her ears, but nothing could block out the drumming sound of the rain. It continued to pour in long, steady streams for about five minutes, then just as she was about to give up hope of seeing Scott, it suddenly let up.

She sensed the change and jumped off the bed to begin pulling on her jogging clothes. When the phone rang at nine forty-five, she rushed to answer it. Emily was sure that it was Scott, and her spirits soared.

"Hello?" She tried to keep her excitement from showing when she answered the phone.

"Emily? Hi! I just found out about Jonathan and Fiona breaking up, and had to call. Is she okay? You should have told me what happened. I could have helped." It wasn't Scott. It was Laurie. Emily had to hide her disappointment.

"I'm sorry. We didn't want to spoil your party."

"What about you? You looked as if you were having a good time with Scott," Laurie said in a sly voice. "Too bad you had to leave early."

"It was a great party."

"Thanks. But tell me what happened between Fiona and Jonathan?"

"There's nothing to tell. They broke up."

"Do you think I should call her?"

"That's up to you. I've got to get off now. I'm expecting another call."

"Anyone I know?"

Emily ignored her. "Listen. I really gotta go, Laurie. 'Bye." She hung up the phone and looked at the clock. It was exactly five minutes after ten.

The next two calls were for her mother. And then the phone rang at ten-thirty. It was Emily's grandparents, calling from Florida. By ten forty-five Scott still hadn't called, and she decided he might not have been able to get through. Either that or he figured the weather was too iffy to go jogging. And if he wasn't going to run, there was no reason to call.

Emily hesitated. Why not call him? If someone came to her asking advice, that's exactly what she would tell *them* to do. She looked up Scott's number in the telephone directory and slowly began punching out his number. But after six rings there was no answer, so she hung up. Scott wasn't even home!

"I'm going for a run in the park," she called out to her parents as she pulled on a sweat shirt. Suddenly she had to get out of the house.

Emily started jogging the minute she hit the sidewalk, and immediately felt a little better. She didn't want to think about why she hadn't heard from Scott as she zig-zagged down tree-lined streets and past large houses. The wind whisked around her, tossing her hair back, and fanning her cheeks. By the time she reached the park, her muscles were warmed up, and her mind was clear.

On impulse, she followed the jogging path toward the long, winding hill that led to the view of the Potomac. It was the perfect day for her to run the entire park, including hills. The weather was cool, and she felt as if she could run forever. The only other time she had ever jogged around the entire park was when she had run with Scott, and she'd only done it then because she didn't want to admit she usually took the cut-off by the lake.

Suddenly thoughts of him came tumbling back, and she began to feel miserable. Last night when Scott had said he would call her, her heart had soared. She got the feeling he really liked her and wanted to be with her. So what happened?

All sorts of thoughts crowded into her brain, but the one that hurt the most was the thought of Heather. Maybe that's where Scott was — at Heather's house. Emily couldn't think of a better reason why Scott wouldn't have called.

Again trying to force thoughts of Scott from her mind, she picked up her pace and took in a deep breath. She wasn't going to let herself take the easy way out today. She was going to run up that hill in record time.

She took off her sweat shirt and tied it in a double knot around her waist. The only sound other than the rustling of the trees in the wind was the angry tapping of her feet against the ground. She picked up the pace even more as soon as she neared the long, winding hill, and with her arms pumping, followed the jogging path around a large playing field.

The hill was in front of her now, and as she started up she leaned forward, with her head tilted down. She didn't want to see how much further she still had to run. She wanted to concentrate on keeping her pace steady and her breathing even. When she got to the steepest part, her breathing came short and fast, and her legs began to feel like lead weights. Even her arms began to ache. She forced herself to keep on going, determined to make it up the hill without walking.

She was almost at the top when she heard another jogger coming from behind her. Judging by the steady pounding of steps against the ground, whoever it was was moving fast. Emily didn't dare look back for fear of slowing down. Instead, a surprising urge to get to the top of the hill took over, and she dug deep down for that extra push and picked up her pace.

"Shorten your stride a little. You'll never set a world record running like that."

Startled, Emily turned to look at Scott as he pulled up alongside her.

"Here, watch me," he said, and raced ahead a few yards."

Emily watched his legs move in short, quick steps and tried to do the same. Scott had a way of making running uphill look easy.

"That's better," he said circling back to her. "Feel the difference?"

She nodded. Scott was right, shortening her stride did make it easier. What she didn't understand was what he was doing there. Maybe he had decided to go jogging alone, and having met up with her, decided to make the best of an awkward situation. She remembered he was a master at putting people at ease, and she flashed him a suspicious stare.

"And another thing, don't lean so far forward. A little lean is okay, but you've practically got your nose to the ground."

Emily automatically straightened up a little, forgetting to be mad at him.

"Not bad," Scott said running alongside her. "Now how come you didn't wait for me?"

His question was so unexpected, Emily's legs stopped moving. She began to pant, and with her hands on her hips, looked him straight in the eye for the first time. "I did," she said between sharp inhalations. "I even called your house, but no one was home." Emily forced her eyes away from Scott and continued running up the hill. He followed her.

"My parents went to play tennis this morning, and I must have already been on my way over to your place," Scott said simply. "Every time I dialed your number I got a busy signal, so I decided to ride over instead. When I got there your mother told me you had already left."

They had reached the top of the hill, but Emily hardly noticed. She was amazed to learn Scott had come to her house, and her heart, which was already beating fast, seemed to speed up even more. She looked over at Scott who was right beside her and their eyes locked. Without speaking she could tell that he was as relieved as she that the whole thing had been explained.

"What now?" Scott said softly.

Emily smiled. "We could run until we drop. I was planning to do the entire park today."

"No kidding? I'm impressed," he said and started to pick up the pace.

For a few moments neither of them spoke. The wind had picked up and Emily was afraid if it blew any harder it would carry her away. She glanced over at Scott and saw him look up at the sky.

"Uh-oh. Looks like it's going to pour any second."

Emily followed his gaze and saw dark circles rapidly moving in over the Potomac. "Think we should try to head for shelter?"

"Nope."

"What then?"

"Get wet," Scott said, the beginning of a playful smile on his lips.

At first, the thought of finishing her run in sopping wet clothes and sneakers seemed immensely unappealing. But as the first drop of rain fell from the sky and landed squarely on her nose, she felt a rush of excitement at doing something she wouldn't normally do.

"Maybe we *should* look for shelter," Scott said as the clouds opened, soaking them instantly.

"Too late!" Emily threw her head back to let the rain dance against her face.

Scott looked at her as if she were crazy. Then with a low, relaxed chuckle, he threw an arm around her and tilted his face up to the sky. Together they started spinning around with their arms out wide and their mouths open, trying to catch the raindrops.

Finally, Emily turned to Scott, panting and dripping and said, "I'll race you to the water fountain." She took off across the field, running as fast as she could.

In a moment Scott caught up with her. He grabbed hold of her sweat shirt and spun her around into his arms. His face was inches away from her own, and she knew he was going to kiss her. She wanted him to, and she closed her eyes, waiting. But before she was able to feel the warmth of his lips against hers, a streak of lightning illuminated the dark sky.

Scott pulled away quickly and took hold of her

hand. "C'mon, we're getting out of here before we're roasted like marshmallows."

The moment was lost, but Emily stifled her disappointment as she followed Scott out of the park.

Chapter
10

"Look, Scott. Everyone's staring at us," Emily said as she and Scott walked hand in hand down the street. Each time a car passed, the passengers would gawk at them through fogged-up windows.

"They want to know what two idiots would walk in the pouring rain," he said with a laugh. "Does it bother you?"

"Who, me?" Emily shook her head, sending wet strands of hair swinging around her face. "The way we look right now, no one is going to recognize us, anyway."

"Are you sure?"

"I'm sure." Emily laughed.

The rain, still falling in soft, even sheets, had drenched her hair completely, and the yellow T-shirt she wore hung wet and limp from her shoulders.

Scott reached over to gently brush a wet strand

of hair away from her mouth. "You look okay to me, Emily Stevens."

"Yeah, sure," she said, wiping drops of rain from her nose and her cheeks. "I believe that."

"You do. Take my word for it." He let go of her hand and pulled her against his side.

Emily let her head rest on his shoulder and they walked that way in silence for a few moments. She couldn't remember feeling so relaxed and happy. Wrapped in her thoughts, with Scott's strong arm around her, she didn't see Jeremy and Diana drive up until the blue Saab slowed down beside them.

Jeremy rolled down his window. "Hey there, Emily, Scott. You guys need a lift?"

Scott looked at Emily and laughed. "So much for not being recognized, eh?"

Jeremy opened his door and leaned forward as they climbed into the Saab. As soon as they sat down, Diana turned to face them from the front seat. "You guys are crazy to go jogging in this weather."

"Certifiably nuts," Scott agreed.

"Yeah, you and my sister," Jeremy said, turning the corner onto Fairview.

"How is Fiona?" Emily asked, leaning forward in her seat.

Jeremy tightened his fingers around the steering wheel and shook his head. "I have no idea. When I knocked on her door this morning, she refused to let me in. I think she's afraid that if I see how miserable she is, I'll start horning in on her love life again."

Emily patted him gently on the shoulder. "Stop worrying about her so much. She can take care of herself."

"Is that your advice, counselor?" Jeremy teased. Then suddenly he turned serious. "I'm just scared Fiona's going to crawl into a hole like she did when she first came to Rose Hill."

"I don't think you have to worry about that." Emily sat back. "Fiona has too many friends now. She also has her dancing."

"Yeah. And that's what got her into this mess with Jonathan."

"Sometimes people are forced to make choices they don't want to," Emily told him. "It isn't Fiona's fault that opening night and the prom are both that Saturday."

Jeremy thought about that as he pulled up in front of Emily's house. "Maybe you could explain that to Jonathan." He looked at her in the rearview mirror.

"Jeremy!" Diana glanced at him. "You promised you wouldn't interfere in Fiona's life again, remember?"

"Yeah. Yeah." He shook his head and the corners of his mouth turned up sheepishly. "I know, but I can't help it. I'm her brother!"

"So?" Diana smiled.

"All right, I give up. Don't talk to Jonathan." He shrugged in defeat. "But see if you can get Fiona to talk to him."

Emily laughed as Jeremy slid out of the car and pulled the seat forward. The rain had let up and all that was coming down now was a light, soft drizzle.

"Think about it, will you?" he said as Emily climbed out of the car. "Fiona will listen to you. She trusts your judgment."

Scott climbed out of the car behind Emily.

"Hey! Where are you going?" Jeremy asked. "Don't you want me to drive you home, too?"

"No, thanks. I've got my bike." Scott turned back to the car. "See you, Di."

"Suit yourself." Jeremy grinned, climbed back into the car, and drove off.

"How did your bike get here?" Emily asked as Jeremy's tail lights disappeared around the corner.

"I rode it over when I came to pick you up this morning."

"Oh. I forgot." She blushed. "Do you want to come in and dry off a little before you ride home? My mother made some terrific soup yesterday, and I can make some hot chocolate."

"Sounds great, but I've got to get home to finish that floor plan, or we won't have anything to show Mr. Barker tomorrow."

He walked over to the side of the house where his blue ten-speed was leaning and lifted the kick stand with his foot. "I'll see you tomorrow afternoon in the student activities room." He started to wheel the bike down the driveway.

There was a big puddle at the edge of the curb and when he stepped into it, his sneaker disappeared under water. He looked up at Emily with a silly, embarrassed shrug. " 'Bye," he called and threw his right leg over the bike.

She giggled and waved. " 'Bye."

Scott started to peddle off. "See you tomorrow."

"Okay," Emily said.

She watched him coast down the hill, and when he was halfway down he looked back once more. She waved again. There was no doubt in her mind. She was in love.

Emily took the stairs two at a time, and the minute she entered her room she peeled off her wet clothes. She did a little dance in the middle of the rug and went over to the closet to get her bathrobe. Gathering her clothes in one hand she headed for the shower, all the time thinking of Scott. Emily couldn't believe she felt so wonderful. She'd had crushes on boys before, but they never amounted to anything. Usually she was busy listening to their love problems and giving out advice. Because she had a reputation for being a good listener, the boys knew she could be trusted and they always wound up becoming her pals.

But she could tell things were going to be different with Scott. Remembering the way he looked at her just before the lightning struck filled her with a light, airy feeling that she could barely contain. She wanted to shout with joy, and she couldn't wait to hop into the shower and sing at the top of her lungs.

As she reached the bathroom door, she heard footsteps on the stairs.

"Hi," Elise called out cheerfully. "Your mother said you were up here." She was dressed in a pair of worn Levi's and a bright pink sweat shirt.

"Oh, hi. I was just going to take a shower."

Elise shrugged and followed Emily into the bathroom. "Wait until you hear what happened when Ben and I went downtown this morning to hit the stores for donations," she bubbled. "You know the stationery store next to Hanson's dress shop, the one run by the sweet gray-haired lady, Mrs. Burger, and her husband?" Elise paused to hike herself up on the counter. "Well, they've decided to retire and they're moving to Florida in June."

"And. . . ?" Emily set her wet clothes on top of the hamper and began to brush her hair. It was still damp and knotted from the rain.

"They were going to have a big 'going out of business' sale to get rid of their inventory. But when we told them about the carnival, they decided to donate half of their inventory to us." She barely paused for a breath. "I'm talking stuffed animals, stationery, pens, pencils, T-shirts, you name it."

"You sure you didn't bribe them?" Emily joked.

"Almost. I invited them to the carnival, but they're going to be away that weekend."

Emily knew Elise was serious. She was the champion of the do-gooders. If she thought it would make the Burgers happy to be invited to the carnival, that's exactly what she would do — invite them.

"Wait, there's more!" Elise reached out to grab Emily's wrist when she went to turn on the shower. "The pet shop is donating thirty goldfish and glass bowls for the carnival."

Emily rolled her eyes and laughed. "You nut! We're never going to use up all these prizes."

"I know that! Ben and I already told the

Burgers that whatever prizes we have left over we'd give to Garfield House, in their name. Don't you think that was a good idea?" she said, grinning.

"You really are something else. Does Tony Martinez know about this windfall?"

"He will soon. Ben got hold of Jonathan and Marc, and they're going to meet him at the stationery store. Then after they help Mr. and Mrs. Burger pack up their inventory, they're going over to Garfield House."

"How's Jonathan? Did Ben say?" Emily asked, grabbing a towel from the linen closet.

Elise shrugged and slid off the counter. "Not too good. Ben's going to try and talk to him."

Emily turned on the shower and Elise started to leave the room.

"I'll see you downstairs," she said. "Your mother invited me to stay for lunch. I'll go help her set the table or something." She closed the door behind her.

Chapter
11

Emily woke earlier than usual on Monday morning, anxious to get to school in the hope that she might see Scott before classes started. She slipped into her favorite pink T-shirt dress and turned to face the full-length mirror on her closet door. Her hair fell in silky waves around her shoulders, and her cheeks were bright with excitement at the thought of seeing him again. She was surprised to see she didn't look any different from the day before. For some reason, she thought being in love might have transformed her overnight.

She rummaged through her drawers for her gold belt and finding it, fastened it loosely around her waist. If only her insides were as calm as she appeared on the outside.

When she finally made it down to the kitchen, Emily realized she had spent too much time in front of the mirror. If she didn't want to be late for school, she would have to hurry. She gulped down a glass of orange juice, called good-bye to her parents, grabbed her book bag and a sweater, and ran out the door.

Just as she reached the school steps, the warning bell rang, and she saw Elise heading her way.

"Hi, Em. What's the special occasion? Today isn't your birthday."

"No special occasion," Emily said with a shrug, turning down the hall toward her locker. "I just felt like wearing a dress for a change."

She adjusted her belt and began turning her combination. Elise grabbed her by the arm.

"Here comes Jonathan," she whispered, and Emily spotted him brushing past a group of students standing in the middle of the corridor. "He looks positively bummed-out."

Emily peered around the edge of her locker door to get a better look. Jonathan had his hat pulled down over his forehead, as if he was hoping no one would notice him, and there was a sadness in his gray eyes.

"You're right. He does look awful," she said when he walked right by them without saying hello. "You would think Fiona broke up with *him*, instead of the other way around. How was he yesterday? Did Ben say?"

"The same." Elise shook her head. "He's taking this whole thing pretty hard."

"So is Fiona."

"No kidding? When did you speak to her? I tried calling after I left your house, but her mother said she was out."

"She was probably at Kim's house talking to Mrs. Barrie," Emily told her.

Elise's eyebrows shot up. "Good for her! It doesn't help any to sit around feeling sorry for yourself. Believe me, I know from experience. When Ben started acting real crazy last Christmas, trying to figure out how he felt about me, I was miserable. But I didn't stop working on the Rollerthon." She looked up sheepishly. "I just cried a lot."

Emily smiled. "Maybe the meeting this afternoon will cheer him up. You know, give him something else to think about besides Fiona." She slammed her locker closed.

Elise sighed. "I hope you're right. I can't stand seeing him look so down."

"Yeah, I know what you mean. I've got to run," Emily said after watching Jonathan walk stiffly down the hall. "If I don't hurry I'll be late for Baylor's history class." She started towards the stairs.

"Okay. See you later," Elise shrugged, and headed off in the opposite direction.

Jonathan was sitting on a bench, leaning forward on his elbows with his chin in his hands when Emily walked onto the quad fourth period. She couldn't see his face, but his posture advertised his mood. She walked over to him and tapped his arm gently. "You look like you could use some company. Want to talk?"

He looked up at her and gave a weak smile. "There's nothing to talk about." He sat back and jammed his hands into his pockets.

Emily didn't move and for a few moments it was very quiet. Jonathan pressed the heel of his hand against his forehead. "I'm sorry. I'm just a mess, Emily. How's Fiona?"

"Not much better than you," Emily told him honestly.

He stared at her. "Ben told me you took her home from the party. Thanks."

"No problem."

Jonathan leaned forward on his arms again and stared at the ground.

"Okay, I can take a hint." Emily shifted her book bag onto the other shoulder. "I'll be sitting on the bench under the cherry tree, reviewing my science notes, if you decide you want to talk. I have a sneaky feeling Miss Zinn is going to spring a surprise quiz on us today." She started to walk away, but Jonathan put a hand on her arm and looked at her with a sense of urgency.

"Emily, has anyone asked you to the prom?"

She turned to him and frowned. "Not yet. Why?"

He shrugged. "I thought if you didn't have a date, you might want to go with me." He looked down at his hands.

For a moment Emily didn't know what to say. She was flattered by the invitation, and liked Jonathan — as a friend. But the only person she really wanted to go to the prom with was Scott. Still, she couldn't bring herself to say no to him outright. She didn't want to make him feel worse by turning him down.

She put her hand on his arm. "Can I let you know tomorrow?" she asked softly.

Jonathan nodded. "Yeah, sure. I can wait."

"Thanks." She dropped her arm. "I'll see you at the meeting." She started to go.

"I won't be there," he called after her. "I have to go over the seating arrangement for the prom."

Emily knew that wasn't the real reason, but gave him a nod anyway. "All right. Talk to you tomorrow." She headed over to the bench.

Later that afternoon, Emily walked into the student activities room and spotted Fiona standing off by herself. She was about to go over and speak to her when Dee grabbed her by the arm.

"Come see the floor plan for the carnival," she said pulling Emily toward the table. A bunch of juniors were already crowding around it, admiring Scott's work.

Emily squeezed in and looked down at the floor plan. Everything was scaled to size and clearly labeled, each booth marked for position. "Has Mr. Barker seen this yet?"

"Yep. First thing this morning," Scott said from behind her.

Emily's heart leaped at the sound of his voice and she looked over her shoulder to smile at him. His eyes met hers and seemed to twinkle as they shared the silent memory of their jog in the rain.

"Mr. Barker wanted to know if Scott would redesign his office," Marc teased.

"Cool it, Harrison." Scott elbowed him. "He approved of everything except for the kissing booth. We have to move it because it's blocking a fire exit."

Emily turned back to the table. "Will that be a problem?"

"Not really." He leaned forward, his arm brushing hers, sending a chill up her spine. "I figure we can move it to the center of the gym. Right here." He pointed to an open area.

"Looks good to me. Are you sure it will fit?"

"Tell you in a sec." Scott reached into his shirt pocket and pulled out a pencil and small ruler. With quick movements he measured the size of the booth, and the center of the gym. "No problem," he smiled. "Want me to pencil it in?"

"Sure."

"Look!" Elise giggled once he had finished. "Scott drew hearts inside the kissing booth. And wait! There's one with our name on it, Ben."

"Let me see that!" He pulled her away from the table to get a closer look. His face was a picture of concentration as he studied the rendering. "I don't see any names on the hearts," he growled after a careful inspection, and everyone burst out laughing.

"Where is our fearless leader?" Marc asked. "It's after three-thirty."

Emily turned to him. "I, uh, don't think Jonathan is coming," she said softly, and saw Fiona's head drop. Emily knew the only reason she had forced herself to show up at the meeting was so she could see him.

For a moment there was an awkward silence as all eyes turned in Fiona's direction. It was obvious that everyone knew she and Jonathan were no longer a couple.

"Okay, we're wasting time. Does anyone have

anything to report?" Emily asked quickly.

Elise spoke up first, telling everyone about Mr. and Mrs. Burger's generous donation. Then one by one the others gave their reports. Finally it was Fiona's turn.

She looked up. "I saw Mrs. Barrie yesterday, and she agreed to be in charge of the catering. But I won't be able to help her contact other parents. I'm going to be pretty busy the next two weeks. Is anyone here willing to take my place?"

"Elise and I can call parents," Ben volunteered unexpectedly. "We've already gotten all the prizes we need, so we'll haxe extra time."

"Thanks, Ben," Fiona said. "I'll call Mrs. Barrie and tell her you and Elise will be filling in for me."

When the meeting was over and everyone started drifting out, Emily hung back, reviewing the notes she'd just taken while Scott rolled up his floor plan and stuffed it inside a long cardboard tube. She couldn't believe how much progress they had made in such a short time. Now that Scott's floor plan had been approved, they could start thinking about decorations for the gym.

She leaned her elbow on the table and rested her chin in her hand. Suddenly Scott leaned over and gently squeezed her arm.

"I'm really impressed with your floor plan," she said, smiling up at him. "You're very talented."

"Thanks. So are you."

Emily laughed. "At what — doodling?"

"Yeah." Scott tightened his hold on Emily's

101

arm and slowly pulled her to her feet until their eyes locked. The next thing Emily knew, Scott was kissing her, a long gentle kiss that made her feel like she was floating on a cloud. She brought her arms up and clasped them around his neck as he pulled her closer.

"Excuse me for interrupting." A voice as cool as cut glass carved into Emily's enchantment. "But Scott, you did say to pick you up at four-thirty, didn't you?"

Emily tore herself away from Scott and felt her face flush with humiliation. Heather Richardson was standing in the doorway, her posture a mixture of smugness and controlled amusement.

Scott looked up, annoyed. "Right. I forgot, sorry." He hit the table lightly with his fist and walked stiffly over to pick up his floor plan. "Give me a sec. I have to drop this off in Barker's office." He headed for the door without so much as a glance in Emily's direction.

Heather moved aside just enough for Scott to slip past her, and as he did, she smiled at him sweetly. Once he had left the room, she turned to face Emily. "You certainly know how to have a good time at your meetings, don't you?"

Emily, her pulse still racing from the kiss, didn't answer. Instead, she picked up her book bag and rummaged around in it.

"You know if I'd known these meetings weren't all work, I might have volunteered to help." Heather leaned forward and winked. "Unfortunately, it's too late now." She held up her long, manicured fingernails for a careful inspection. "I have a million things to do before the prom. I'm

102

having my dress custom-made at Rezato's and I have to go shopping for jewelry and shoes. Of course, you know Scott and I are going to the prom together?"

Emily felt her heart stop beating. "You are?" she gasped.

Heather nodded. "Mm-hmmm. Don't tell me Scott hasn't told you?"

A sharp pain jabbed at Emily's heart now, and she suddenly found it very hard to breathe. She could never face Scott now. Snatching up her book bag she fled from the room.

"Where's Emily?" Scott asked when he came back and saw she wasn't there.

Heather slid off the table and walked up to him, stopping when she was just inches away.

"She left."

Scott looked at her suspiciously. "Why?"

"Oh, I don't know." She reached out to touch his shirt and gently ran her fingertips along his collar. "I think she was upset when I told her you and I are going to the prom together."

"Huh?"

Heather didn't miss a beat. "Don't you remember? I asked you to take me if Danny Fisher didn't invite me? Well, he's taking some dumb sophomore, so you and I have a date."

Scott looked at Heather, not sure he had heard her correctly. "What did you say?"

"You and I are going to the prom together." She smiled at him sweetly.

"No, wait! I can't. . . ." Scott gulped.

"But you promised." Heather's voice became a whine.

"Yeah, well this is one promise I may have to break." Scott spun around toward the door and took off down the hall. He had to catch up with Emily and tell her this was all a big mistake. As usual, he hadn't been paying attention to Heather when she asked him to take her to the prom. Otherwise he never would have gotten himself into this mess. It was his own fault. Scott just hoped he hadn't blown it with Emily.

Chapter
12

Emily pushed open the wide double door and raced across the quad as Heather's words played over and over in her head. Scott had purposely led her on when all the time he still cared for Heather. How could she have been so blind? The only reason he had been so affectionate and warm to Emily this weekend was because he couldn't be with *her*. Heather's grandparents were visiting for the weekend. Isn't that what Scott had told Bart at the party?

She collapsed on the wooden bench when she got to the bus stop and buried her face in her hands. She didn't care who saw her crying. A terrible sense of unfairness engulfed her, and she couldn't hold her tears in any longer. No wonder everyone had been so surprised when they saw her with Scott Saturday night. They all knew about him and Heather. Why didn't anyone warn her?

Emily's stomach clenched painfully. She felt so

foolish. Because she was in love with Scott — more in love than she had ever been in her entire life — she'd been too blind to see what was going on. All she had noticed was how easy it was to be with Scott.

A sob burst from her lips, followed by another and another. When the bus finally pulled up, Emily boarded and slid into the first empty seat she came to. The lady behind her offered her a tissue, which she took gratefully. She blew her nose and dabbed at her eyes, then turned to gaze out the window as the bus drove past Kennedy High.

In the distance she thought she saw Scott running across the empty quad, and fresh tears began running down her cheeks. She let them flow, and by the time the bus pulled to a stop at the bottom of her hill, Emily's face felt as if it might crack, and her body felt drained, as if she had just run a marathon.

Half in a daze she walked up the hill to her house. The minute she got inside, she quickly ran upstairs to bathe her face in cold water.

Less than five minutes later there was a knock in the bathroom door. "Emily, there's a phone call for you."

She lifted the cold washcloth from her eyes and stared into the mirror. "Can you take a message, Mom?" She didn't feel like talking to anyone right now. She just wanted to be left alone.

She heard her mother's footsteps disappear down the stairs as she reached for the towel to dry her face. A few minutes later when she came out of the bathroom, her mother called to her from the kitchen. "It was Scott, dear. He left his number and asked that you call him back."

Emily hesitated. Why was he calling her? What could he possibly want? Hadn't he hurt her enough already? She dragged herself back to her room, shut the door behind her, and flopped down onto her bed. It didn't matter. There was no way she was going to call him back. She couldn't. Not now. Not when she felt so humiliated she wanted to die.

Emily tried to act normal in school the next day, even though she felt like she might burst out crying any moment. She still couldn't understand what had happened with Scott, but she was determined not to let the unfortunate incident with Heather interfere with her school work or with the planning for the senior carnival. She dreaded the moment she would have to face Scott again, but at least there wasn't another committee meeting until the following week. By then she hoped to be able to act as if the whole ugly episode had never happened.

So far she had made it through history and French without spacing out, and now she was on her way to third-period English class. As she passed by the chemistry lab, Jonathan stepped out. He looked about as unhappy as she felt.

"Hi," he said in a flat voice when he spotted her in the crowd. "How's it going?"

"Okay." Emily shrugged.

"You heading toward the west staircase?"

"Uh-huh. I've got English with Miss Cook next."

"I'll walk you." He stuffed his hands into his pockets.

Emily gave a half nod and continued down the hall. One or two heads turned to look at them and she wondered what they were looking at. She laughed when the thought occurred to her. She and Jonathan must be an amusing sight, the happiest couple around. He felt betrayed by Fiona, and she had fallen in love with a guy only to find out he was seeing someone else.

When they reached the west staircase, Jonathan stopped and looked down at the floor. "Uh, Emily." He cleared his throat. "Do you have an answer for me yet?"

She looked at him in confusion. What was he talking about? Then it came to her — the prom. She'd forgotten all about Jonathan's invitation.

"I'm sorry. I forgot. . . ."

"Yeah. I figured," he interrupted sadly.

"Wait, you didn't let me finish." She shook her head and sighed. Twenty-four hours ago she was almost sure she and Scott would be going to the prom together. But since then things had changed. Did that mean she had to sit home alone next Saturday when she could be having a marvelous time? She'd just about decided being miserable was no fun, and that she'd already had her fill of it. "I would love to go to the prom with you," she told him.

Jonathan looked at her with surprise. "You would?" He let out a deep breath. "That's great. I don't know who else I could have asked."

"But I am going to have to tell Fiona," Emily

added and saw Jonathan flinch. "She's still my friend."

"Sure. I understand," Jonathan answered moodily before backing into the stairwell.

Emily headed down the hall, her spirits uplifted. She now had something else to think about besides Scott. She only hoped Fiona wouldn't be upset when she told her she'd accepted Jonathan's invitation to the prom.

She turned the corner trying to figure out if she had anything in her closet to wear and came to a sudden stop. Scott was leaning uncomfortably against the wall right outside her English class, his eyes shifting impatiently from his watch to the hallway and back again.

She hesitated for a moment, wondering how she could avoid him, but Scott looked up and saw her.

"Emily! Hey, Emily!"

He started weaving his way toward her, and as she watched him approach, she felt a huge lump rise in her throat. What did Scott want? Was he going to tell her how sorry he was for humiliating her in front of Heather? She couldn't handle that. She'd burst into tears.

She immediately spun around and started walking back the way she had come. She realized she was now heading away from her English class, but she had to get away from Scott before she made a complete fool of herself.

"Emily, wait!" He yelled louder this time.

She rounded the corner and slipped into the stairwell Jonathan had taken moments ago. She was behaving like a real nut case, running away like this. It certainly wasn't what she would advise someone else to do. But it was easier to give advice than follow it. She grabbed hold of the railing and started racing down the stairs. She didn't have to look back to know Scott was right behind her. She could hear his footsteps getting closer, and the moment she reached the ground floor, she felt the touch of his hand on her arm.

"Wait, please," Scott pleaded when she pulled away.

"What for?" Emily responded tersely.

"I need to talk to you."

"Go ahead. Talk." She didn't stop walking.

"How can I when you won't stand still?"

Emily stopped and shot him an angry glare. She pushed back her thick, dark hair and adjusted the gold bracelet on her wrist.

"Okay," he sighed. "For starters, didn't your mother tell you I called yesterday?"

"Yes, she told me," Emily snapped.

"Then why didn't you call back?" He looked shocked. "I just about went crazy waiting."

"Really? That's too bad." She started walking again.

"C'mon, Em, give me a break." Scott ran in front of her and put his arms out to cut her off. "How do you expect me to have a serious conversation with you if you keep racing down the hall?"

"I don't."

"At least let me explain about Heather."

"Why bother? I'm really not interested."

Scott ran his fingers through his hair as if he

was trying to figure out what to say next. "Look, I know you're upset about what happened, but I swear, it's not what you think. I barely know Heather. We're not even friends."

"Sure," Emily answered. "That's why you're taking her to the prom." There was an unexpected tug at the back of her throat.

Scott looked a little embarrassed. "I can explain that, too."

"You don't have to. It just so happens that I'm going to the prom with Jonathan."

Scott stared at her, unexpected hurt in his eyes, and for a fleeting moment she was tempted to reach out to him. Then she reminded herself that Scott had led her on, and that he hadn't even denied he was taking Heather to the prom.

"Jonathan Preston asked you to the prom?" he finally said. "When?"

"Yesterday, *before* the meeting."

Scott nodded. "I see." He stuck his hands into his pockets and abruptly turned away.

Emily stared moodily into space. Everything had gone wrong. She had wanted to hurt Scott by showing him that their kiss had been as meaningless to her as it must have been to him. Only now that she had drawn the lines of defense, instead of feeling protected, she felt miserable.

Emily wasn't the only one who felt miserable. As Scott walked away, his head began to pound. He almost turned back, but just then the last bell rang, and he knew it was too late. Emily would have already taken off for her English class.

Scott continued down the hall, not really

headed anywhere special. He didn't feel like going to the quad because there would be too many people there, so he kept walking straight ahead until he came to the student council bulletin board. He stopped to read the notices:

SENIOR POETRY ASSEMBLY
TUESDAY 4TH PERIOD

"Hey, do you have a pass?"

Scott looked up and saw Mr. Armand, one of the hall monitors, walking toward him.

"No. I'm on my way to the student activities room," Scott told him impulsively. "This is my study period."

Mr. Armand nodded. "Okay, hurry up then."

Scott turned right. He now had a destination and a purpose. If Jonathan was in the student activities room he would try to find out if there was anything behind his asking Emily to the prom.

When he opened the door, he found Jonathan alone in the student activities room. He was sitting at the table with his head between his hands, staring down at a sheet of paper.

"You busy?" Scott asked.

Jonathan looked up and sighed. "Oh, hi." He rubbed his forehead with one hand. "What's up?"

Scott pushed up the sleeves of his rugby shirt and walked over to him. "Nothing really. I was just talking to Emily Stevens, and she mentioned you two were going to the prom together," he said slipping into a seat opposite him.

"Yeah." Jonathan nodded. "I wasn't about to miss the biggest event of the school year." He

112

folded his arms across his chest. "Besides, I've always liked Emily."

Scott shifted in his chair. "So there's something going on between you?"

"Could be." Jonathan shrugged. "As far as I know she isn't seeing anyone special, and since Fiona and I are finished. . . ."

Scott nodded uncomfortably. He was beginning to get a knot in the middle of his chest.

"Hey, anyone here see my sister?" Jeremy Stone stuck his head through the doorway, and saw Jonathan flinch at his mention of Fiona. "Sorry." He shook his head in disgust, "I have this habit of saying the wrong thing at the wrong time."

"Forget it," Jonathan said. "Have you tried the quad?"

Jeremy shook his head. "I'm heading there now."

"Wait, I'll walk with you." Scott got up to leave. He suddenly felt the urge to run. "I'm going to do a few laps around the track"

After third period, Emily headed for the auditorium. There was a special poetry assembly today, with Phoebe Hall and some other seniors reading the works of famous American poets. Since the entire school had to be there, Emily knew she would see Fiona.

She entered the auditorium and spotted Elise seated in an aisle seat, waving. In the same row was Ben, with his nose in a book, and farther in beside two empty seats, were Jonathan and Matt Jacobs, busy talking.

113

"Have you seen Fiona?" Emily leaned over to whisper into Elise's ear.

Elise twisted around in her seat and started searching the auditorium. It was mobbed with kids milling around the aisles. "I thought I saw her walk in a few minutes ago."

Emily joined her in surveying the audience and spotted Woody parading down the aisle. But before he got to her, he found three empty seats in the middle of a row and started motioning wildly to Kim and Sasha.

"There she is," Elise pointed a moment later. "The next aisle over, near the front. She's sitting with Jeremy and Diana."

Emily strained her neck to see where she was pointing and spotted Fiona. "Thanks," Emily said to Elise. "I'll fill you in on everything later."

She wove her way down the aisle until she got to the fifth row. Fiona was seated all the way at the other end, but it would be easier to squeeze by everyone in the row than fight her way through the crowd at the front of the auditorium.

She turned to the person on the aisle to say, "Excuse me," and found herself staring into a pair of blue-gray eyes. It was Scott.

For a moment she just stared at him. His hair was damp from a recent shower, and he was looking at her as if he were searching for something he had lost. It made her throat muscles tighten.

"You want to get by?" He finally stood up.

"Please," Emily answered.

Scott leaned back against his upraised seat and motioned for her to pass.

"Thanks," she said, and somehow managed to squeeze by without touching him.

When she reached the empty seat beside Fiona, she flopped down and closed her eyes to hide her obvious hurt.

Fiona spun around. "Emily, where did you come from?"

"Hi." She opened her eyes. "I have to ask you something, and I want an honest answer. Promise."

"Sure," Fiona answered.

Emily leaned sideways and forced a smile. "It's about the prom," she began. "Jonathan asked me to go with him and I said yes. Is that okay? If not, just say so, and I'll tell Jonathan to forget it. I don't want anything to ruin our friendship."

Fiona's eyes widened and she threw her arms around Emily. "Oh, Em. That's wonderful."

"It is?"

"Of course." Fiona pulled back. "I was so worried Jonathan would wind up asking someone like Heather Richardson just so he would have a date. Once she got her claws into him, she'd never let go."

Emily dropped her eyes. "You don't have to worry about him asking Heather. She's going to the prom with Scott Phillips."

"What!" Fiona stared at her. "I knew there was something going on between the two of them, but I didn't think it was that serious. I mean, he could hardly take his eyes off you at the meeting yesterday. To me, that said he and Heather were history."

"History has a way of repeating itself," Emily said and slid down low in her seat. The lights in the auditorium began to dim, and a moment later, Phoebe strode confidently over to the lecture stand in the center of the stage.

Chapter
13

The first person Emily spotted when she and Jonathan walked into the hotel ballroom was Scott. He was wearing a tuxedo with a simple white shirt and striking red bow tie and cumberbund. His thick blond hair was neatly combed away from his face. It didn't seem possible, but Emily thought he looked more handsome than ever.

A sharp stab of envy shot through her when she saw Heather, in a low-cut, expensive-looking white beaded gown, cuddle up to Scott and whisper something in his ear. He nodded and they started walking toward the terrace where a lot of other kids were standing around talking.

Emily pulled her eyes away from Scott at the same time Dee came up beside her.

"Wow! This place looks fabulous!" Dee said, taking in the ballroom with its high ceilings and tables covered with pink tablecloths and white flower centerpieces. "I wonder if Jonathan knows pink is my favorite color?"

"I don't know." Emily smiled at Dee who looked terrific in her pink strapless gown. "But I love your dress."

"Same here." Dee laughed. Emily had on a shimmery blue satin dress with off-the-shoulder sleeves.

"What is this, the mutual admiration society?" Marc joked.

"Could be." Dee flicked a piece of lint off her dress while Emily did her best to keep her face bright. It wasn't all that easy until she spotted Elise and Ben walking in the door.

Ben looked very uncomfortable in his tuxedo, and kept moving his head as if his shirt collar was too tight. But Elise, as usual, looked great. The hem of her jade green gown swirled delicately around her ankles, and the flowers she had woven into her hair matched those in the corsage she wore on her wrist.

"What did Ben have to say about your dress?" Emily asked after they spotted her and came over.

"Would you believe nothing." Elise scowled. "I swear, one of these days he's going to get it. All he talked about on the way to the hotel was the latest mechanical doodad he's working on. I think it's going to replace the automobile or something."

"Jonathan would tell you how nice you look," Emily teased her. "Go ask him."

"I would, only I don't see him around." Elise looked at Emily. "Do you happen to know where wonder boy has disappeared to?"

Emily glanced over toward the stage. "He said

he wanted to talk to the band leader when we first walked in, but I don't see him there." She shrugged. "Knowing Jonathan, he could be anywhere."

"That's our fearless leader," Marc quipped. "The original workaholic."

"Maybe, but he's done one heck of a job organizing the prom," Dee cut in. "Everything looks super."

"Has anyone checked out the terrace?" Ben tugged on his shirt collar. "I understand there's food out there."

Emily shook her head feebly. As long as Scott and Heather were on the terrace there was no way she was going near there.

"Maybe later," she said with false enthusiasm. And no sooner were the words out when Scott came strolling in the door. He spotted Emily standing with the others and turned in their direction. Oh, please don't come over here, Emily prayed.

She was saved when Jonathan walked up. "Time to head over to the table." He gave Emily a crooked smile. "I'm about to announce the prom queen's entrance."

Emily breathed a sigh of relief and followed Elise and Ben to their table while Jonathan made his way over to the stage microphone. The band struck a chord, and a buzz of excitement filled the room.

"Will everyone please stand and welcome our prom queen and her escort," Jonathan's voice echoed throughout the room.

There was a roaring burst of applause as

Diana, resplendent in a pink chiffon gown and delicate silver tiara was escorted into the ballroom by Jeremy. He led her to the center of the dance floor, where they stood in the spotlight until the band started playing. Then they led off the dance.

After a few minutes other couples began joining them, and before long the dance floor was filled with bodies all swaying slowly in time with the music. Emily watched as several people she knew danced by her table. But when she saw Scott and Heather moving in her direction, she turned back to the table and picked up her glass of ice water.

When the band swung into a raucous number, Ben jumped up from his seat and exclaimed, "The leaping lizard!"

"Not with me you don't," Elise sat back in her chair and crossed her arms firmly. "My feet have taken enough of a beating for one evening. Ask Emily."

Ben turned to her. "How about it. Want to risk getting your feet mashed?"

Emily would rather have sat this one out, but Ben was already moving to the music, so she let him pull her onto the dance floor where he immediately started stomping and twisting his body around. He wasn't the best of dancers, but he did seem to enjoy himself a lot and as the music accelerated to a fever pitch, he moved faster and faster.

It took all of Emily's concentration just to keep her feet out of his way. Every now and then he would spin her around wildly, and at one point during the dance he grabbed her around the waist so that her feet were literally off the ground. Just when she thought she might collapse, the lights in the ballroom dimmed, and the band went into a slow dreamy number.

"May I?"

Emily turned around to see Scott holding out his hand, and a tiny gasp of surprise escaped her lips. Her instinct was to stay away from him, but like a magnet she found herself drawn into his outstretched arms. She couldn't fight it, and sliding her hands around his waist, she leaned her head on his shoulder. For a moment they simply stood there, holding each other and letting the soft music surround them. Then Scott drew Emily closer to him and ran his fingers gently across the nape of her neck. Her heartbeat started to quicken, and she felt her stomach do a slow sky dive. It was wonderful to be in Scott's arms again.

"Are you having a good time?" He pulled back a little to look at her.

Emily nodded. "Are you?"

"Right now I am." He gathered her closer again and they went on swaying and holding each other.

"You look very elegant in a tuxedo," Emily said.

Scott gave her an amused grin. "You mean a monkey suit, don't you?"

"Whatever."

Her arms shifted a little around Scott's waist and he smiled down at her with his blue-gray eyes. "You look pretty special yourself."

He let his cheek rest against her hair as he led

her in graceful, light turns around the floor. Heather and Jonathan were the furthest things from her mind. Scott's arms were around her now, and her love for him welled up inside, filling her heart to the breaking point.

"I noticed Jonathan has been pretty busy all evening," Scott said after a few minutes.

"Yes, he's determined not to let anything go wrong tonight."

"You haven't been dancing much."

"I'm dancing now."

"Yes, you are." Scott tightened his arms around her and she snuggled against his soft shirt. Emily closed her eyes, letting her body flow with his movements.

She didn't see Heather standing on the sidelines giving her the fish eye until the music stopped. She opened her eyes and quickly dropped her arms from around Scott's waist.

"Wait, there's going to be another dance, and Jonathan's still not at the table."

"I really don't feel like dancing anymore."

"Okay." Scott released his hold on her and took a step back. "How about a walk out on the terrace?"

Emily looked at him, confused. What was Scott trying to pull? Didn't he see Heather staring at them? She could feel her frustration building. Ever since Laurie's party she'd been getting signals from Scott saying he cared about her. But if he really did like her, why had he asked Heather to the prom?

She didn't have the answer, and she couldn't stand there all night debating the issue. The reality was that Heather, not Emily, was Scott's date tonight.

"Sorry, but I've got to visit the ladies' room." She forced herself to smile, and retreated hastily.

Fiona stepped forward for her fifth bow of the evening. The audience had loved the ballet, and many of the kids were still applauding wildly. She looked out at the sea of young faces, and dropped into another graceful curtsy. She felt wonderful and elated, but amid all the excitement, she found herself wondering what Jonathan was doing at the prom. She had caught a glimpse of her parents in the audience, but it was his face she would have loved to have seen.

She stood up and was about to step back toward the middle of the stage when one of the stage hands came walking out, carrying a bouquet of roses. As he handed them to Fiona, her eyes misted with tears. For a moment she was backstage at Kennedy, before *Oklahoma*! That night she had been given a large bouquet of spring flowers with one red rose in the middle. The single rose had been from Jonathan.

She dabbed at her eyes with the back of her hand and stepped back as the final curtain came down. A moment later the director of the ballet school came running out onto the stage and gave her a big hug. "You were terrific!"

Soon everyone in the cast was hugging and kissing and jumping around the stage. Even the girl who had injured her ankle during rehearsal came limping over to Fiona.

"Congratulations," she said sincerely. "I wish

it could have been me, but I have to admit you made a beautiful Swanilda."

"Thank you," Fiona smiled. "I'm really sorry about your ankle."

"Me, too," the other girl shrugged. "But those are the breaks. It will heal." She limped off to congratulate another dancer.

Fiona watched her go, wondering if a broken heart would heal as easily as an ankle. She had been trying to convince herself lately that what she and Jonathan had between them would survive. They were meant to be together. But tonight, thinking of him at the prom, she wasn't so sure anymore.

She made her way into her tiny dressing room and set the roses down on the makeup table. It was then she first noticed a small card on the flowers, hidden behind the white satin ribbon. She quickly reached in to pull out the note, hoping with all her heart it would be from Jonathan. Instead she noticed Emily's familiar handwriting:

Dear Fiona —
We're thinking of you tonight,
All your friends

Fiona put her hands up to her face and wept.

Meanwhile, halfway across town there was silence in the car as Jonathan drove Emily home. When he pulled up in front of her house, he made no move to get out of the car. Instead he sat staring straight ahead with both hands gripped tightly around the steering wheel. "Emily, I want to apologize for tonight. I know I wasn't the best escort."

Emily shrugged. He could just as easily have been referring to her as a date. After her dance with Scott, she had sat in the ladies' room for almost half an hour, trying to figure out what to make of Scott's behavior. If Elise hadn't gotten worried and come looking for her, she might never have come out. "That's okay. You had a lot of things to take care of."

"But that's not why I wasn't around." He pounded the steering wheel with the palm of one hand. "I knew if I didn't keep busy checking on things, I'd go nuts thinking about Fiona all night. She should have been here with me tonight!"

Emily's heart melted at the pain she heard in his voice and she forgot all about her own problems. "Oh, Jonathan, you know what's wrong with you? You're stubborn. It's obvious you've been miserable ever since you broke up with Fiona, so why don't you just swallow your pride and give her a call."

"It won't change anything." Jonathan took a deep breath. "I love Fiona. But I meant it when I said I was through playing second fiddle. It would be different if Fiona wasn't so single-minded. But all she ever thinks about is her dancing. It takes precedence over everything else in her life, including me."

Emily wanted to help Jonathan see that it wasn't true, but she had to do it tactfully. "You know, you and Fiona are alike in a lot of ways. You both may have different interests, but you're two very dedicated people. Look how hard you worked on the prom because it was important to you. Well, you can't lose sight of the fact that dancing is just as important to Fiona."

Jonathan ran his hand lightly over the steering wheel but said nothing.

"Don't let your pride ruin a good thing," she told him.

"Every relationship has it's rough edges." She swallowed to hold back her tears at the thought of her own fledgling relationship. Emily slipped out of the car and made her way into her house.

Chapter
14

"So, how was opening night?" Emily asked as she munched on a carrot stick. It had to have been better than the prom.

"Oh, Em. It was one of the best nights of my life." Fiona sat with her back against a tree and her bare feet resting on the grass. It was another beautiful spring day and most of the student body was spending lunch period in the quad. "The minute I stepped onto that stage I felt so alive, as if I belonged there, like I had come home."

"That good, eh?" Emily smiled.

Fiona looked over at her and nodded. "The only thing missing was Jonathan. If he had been there, it would have been perfect." Her blue eyes suddenly clouded over.

Emily's heart went out to her friend. "Have you seen him at all today?" she asked delicately.

"I passed him in the hall between second and third period, but he pretended he didn't see me.

It's been that way ever since I told him I couldn't go to the prom. I no longer exist in his life."

"Maybe he really didn't see you."

"Come on, Em." Fiona shook her head sadly. "We practically collided in the middle of the hall. And if that wasn't enough to get him to notice me, Ben, who was walking with him, called out, 'Hi, Fiona,' loud enough to turn heads as we passed."

Emily sighed. She had hoped her talk with Jonathan would knock some sense into him, but apparently he still hadn't completely worked out his feelings. "I know it isn't easy, but give him a little more time. He'll come around." She took another bite of her carrot.

"I don't think so." Fiona leaned her head back against the tree trunk and stared up at the sky. "It's over. I can tell. Why else would Jonathan be ignoring me like this? I just wish it didn't have to hurt so much." She blinked her eyes to stop the tears that threatened to spill down her cheeks.

Emily reached over to put a comforting hand on Fiona's shoulder. "It doesn't have to, because it isn't over between you two. Not by a long shot. Haven't you noticed how spaced-out Jonathan's been since Laurie's party?"

"So. . . ?"

"It's because he still loves you. It's driving him crazy."

"Yeah, sure. Be serious."

"I am being serious. He told me so himself."

Fiona turned around to stare at Emily in disbelief. "When?"

"After the prom." Emily looked her straight in the eye. "You see, Jonathan was acting sort of weird all evening, and when he dropped me off at home he admitted it was because he couldn't stop thinking about you."

Fiona continued to stare at her openmouthed. "Are you serious?"

Emily nodded.

"What else did he say?"

"Oh, all sorts of dumb things, like he's tired of playing second fiddle, and that you care more about your dancing than you do about him. . . ."

"But that's not true!" Fiona gasped.

"Mmmm. You don't have to tell me that." Emily dropped her arm. "And deep down I don't think Jonathan believes it, either. He just isn't ready to admit it."

"Will he ever?"

Emily heard the distress in Fiona's voice and gave her hand a supportive squeeze. "Hang in there, kid." She smiled warmly. "I think you two are a lot alike, and Jonathan's just not used to dealing with someone who's as determined as he is. But he'll come around eventually."

"I hope it's before my last performance. I'd really like him to see me dance in *Coppelia*."

For a moment Emily said nothing. She wasn't one to meddle in other people's affairs, but her mind was turning rapidly. Maybe if Jonathan saw Fiona dance it would help him understand why she had made the decision she did.

She turned to Fiona and smiled. "Are there still tickets available for tonight?" she asked her.

"I'm probably the only one at Kennedy High who hasn't seen you dance. And word has it you're pretty terrific."

Fiona blushed. "If you're serious I can reserve house seats for you."

"You bet I am. I want to see for myself what all this fuss is about," she teased.

"In that case there will be two free tickets waiting for you at the box office. Bring a date."

"I plan to." Emily sat up straight and smiled at her. "And I expect a knock-out performance."

"You'll get one."

"Promise?"

"Promise."

After school Emily walked into the student activities room looking for Jonathan. Now that Fiona had promised to reserve two tickets for her, Emily was determined to go ahead with her plan. All she had to do was get Jonathan to agree to take her out tonight. She opened the door and found a bunch of carnival workers busy making signs for the game booths. Now that the prom was over, plans for the carnival had gone into high gear.

"Hey, Emily! What do you think of this?" Dee held up a sign for the ring toss. "Is the lettering large enough?"

"Perfect," Emily said. "I like the drawing on the side, too."

"Oh, Pam did that." Dee pushed a strand of hair away from her face with a forearm. "Jonathan said he thought the sign could use some color."

"I agree." Emily glanced at the other signs spread out on the table. "They really look great."

"Wait until you see the game booths Scott's building. They'll knock your eyes out!" Ben commented from the corner where he and Pam were painting dozens of milk cartons. It had been decided they would be perfect props for the ring toss and baseball throw booths.

Emily's stomach flipped at the mention of Scott's name. She hadn't seen him since the prom.

"What do you think of Rambo here?" Matt lifted a large cardboard replica of Sylvester Stallone off the table. Instead of a machine gun, he held a red and gold Kennedy High banner in his arms.

"Why did you cut out his face?" Emily poked her finger through the large hole where it should have been.

Matt stood the cardboard figure up in front of him and let his own face fill the hole.

"I hope you're not planning to sucker me into playing Rambo during the carnival," Ben quipped. "A wet sponge in the face is not my idea of fun."

Matt looked at him and chuckled. "You're not going to believe this, but Jonathan got Mr. Barker and Mr. Baylor to agree to be our guinea pigs. And he's working on the vice-principal!"

"Old eagle-eyes actually agreed to let us throw sponges at him?" Ben's eyes widened in disbelief. "The lines are going to be a mile long with kids trying to get back at him for all the miserable hours spent in his study hall — not to mention the lousy history grades he gives out."

"The seniors are going to love that," Dee giggled.

"Why do you think Jonathan asked him to volunteer?" Matt beamed. "Our fearless leader is always thinking."

"But not always clearly," Emily sighed.

"I know what you mean." Dee looked up from the sign she was working on. "He's become a real drag since he broke up with Fiona. I wish they would kiss and make up already."

"Maybe they will now that the prom is over," Emily hinted.

Ben noticed a tiny smile on her lips. "Hey, you look like the cat who swallowed the canary. Do you know something we don't?" he asked.

She shook her head. "Sorry."

"Too bad. I think we're all hoping someone will come up with an idea on how to get those two back together."

"Does anyone know where Jonathan is right now?" Emily asked. "There's something I need to talk to him about. It's important."

"You can try the woodworking shop. He might be helping Scott with the booths," Matt suggested.

"And if he is there, tell him I'll be leaving for Mr. and Mrs. Burger's house at four sharp," Ben added.

"Sure," she said. "I'll catch you guys later."

As Emily rounded the corner she heard loud hammering noises coming from inside the wood-working shop. She hoped Jonathan was there. She didn't feel like running into Scott alone.

She put a nervous hand on the doorknob and opened the door. Sure enough, Scott was the only one in the room.

Emily's fingers tightened around the doorknob. The sight of him bent over a work table nailing two long pieces of board together sent her pulse racing. What should she do? Stay and confront him or inch her way out?

Before she could do anything, Scott stopped his hammering and looked up. When he spotted Emily, a look of genuine surprise stole across his face.

"Emily, hi!" He straightened and wiped his forehead with the back of his hand. "You want to look at some of the game booths?" He pointed to a stack of wooden frames lined up against the wall behind him. "Of course they still have to be nailed together. But we can do that once we get them into the gym." He stood looking at her.

Emily dropped her eyes to the hammer laying on the table by his hand. "Actually I'm looking for Jonathan. Have you seen him around?"

Scott's face clouded over. "Not since lunch." He picked up the hammer and began turning it in his hand.

"Do you have any idea where he might be? It's really important."

"Sorry. I can't help you."

"That's okay," she started to back out the door. "Sorry if I bothered you."

"Wait!" Scott put his hand out and took a step toward her. "Why don't you hang around for a few minutes in case he shows up?"

"You're sure I won't be in the way?"

Scott gave her a crooked smile. "Not if you help by handing me the nails."

Emily stepped into the room and closed the door.

"Sit over there." Scott pointed to a stool next to the worktable, then turned and proceeded to lift two new boards onto the table.

Emily watched him bend over and stretch the tape measure across the boards to mark off measurements before he began nailing them together. His navy sweat shirt stretched tightly across his broad back, while blond hair fell gracefully over his forehead. What was it about Scott that made her melt inside every time she saw him?

"Nail, please," Scott said without looking up.

She picked one out of the box sitting on the table in front of her and held it out to him. "Here."

He put out his hand and their fingers touched briefly. She felt again the warmth of his touch and had to close her eyes. When she opened them again, she found him staring at her in an odd, searching way. She decided she couldn't just sit there so close to him with so many unanswered questions pounding away in her head. She still had no idea why he had ever kissed her, why he had bothered to ask her to dance at the prom, why he had acted like he cared for her when he was so obviously involved with someone else.

"Maybe I'd better go look for Jonathan." She slid off the stool. She had to escape this sinking feeling.

Just then the door swung open and Jonathan walked in. "Hi." He smiled at Emily. "I hear you've been looking for me."

"Jonathan!" Emily's face lit up. "I've got two tickets for tonight and I need a date," she blurted out, unaware of Scott's eyes on her. "Will you go with me?"

Jonathan laughed at her boldness. "I guess so, as long as it won't cost me a fortune. The prom pretty much wiped me out."

Emily let out a sigh of relief. "It won't cost you a penny. I promise. The tickets are on the house."

"No kidding. What are we going to see?"

"Well, I can't say . . . I mean, I want it to be a surprise."

Jonathan gave her a puzzled frown, but she didn't offer any information. Finally he shrugged. "What the heck, you're on. What time do you want me to pick you up?"

"How's seven?" Emily said brightly.

"Okay. I've got to run. Ben's waiting for me in the parking lot. See you guys later." He took off out the door.

Emily turned to tell Scott about her plan to get Fiona and Jonathan back together and swallowed her words. His forehead was tense and his shoulders rigid as he hammered nail after nail into the wood in long, hard drives. She stared at him with a puzzled frown. Why was he suddenly acting so weird?

"Scott?" she walked up to him and rested a gentle hand on his shoulder. He jumped as if he'd been burned. "Is something wrong?"

He gazed up at her with a hurt look in his eyes.

"Do you always go around asking guys out on dates?" His voice sounded edgy.

Emily stiffened slightly. She hadn't expected such curtness and for a moment didn't know what to say. "Only when I have tickets to something special like tonight."

"And how often is that?" Scott scowled as he drove the final nail into the wood.

"What is this, the third degree?" She clasped her arms around her waist and stepped back to give him room to lift up the wooden frame and stack it against the wall with the others.

"Call it whatever you want. I'm curious." He snatched up the box of nails and pitched them into a drawer. He slammed the hammer into place on the peg board.

"About what?"

Scott looked at her icily. "For starters, how serious is it between you and Jonathan Preston?"

Emily laughed. She couldn't believe Scott thought there was something going on between them. Hadn't he noticed how despondent Jonathan had been these past two weeks? "It isn't. We're just friends."

Scott jammed his hands into his pockets and walked over to the window. He was clearly unconvinced. "And I was born yesterday." He stood staring out at the quad.

"But it's true." Emily crossed over to stand beside him. "Why would I lie to you?"

Scott threw back his head and laughed. It was a sad, ironic laugh. "Beats me." He walked stiffly out of the room.

Chapter 15

Emily slunk down onto the stool, her head spinning. She couldn't remember ever being as confused as she was right now. What had gotten into Scott? He was usually so even-tempered. Yet here he was acting like a jealous boyfriend —

She gasped. Was it possible? It seemed crazy, but why else would Scott act so weird? Her heart started to beat wildly. She was suddenly both terrified and elated. The last time she let herself believe Scott was more than just a friend, she wound up looking like a fool. Could his feelings have changed? She drew her eyebrows together as she tried to make sense of his actions. There was only one way to find out.

She jumped up from her chair and raced out of the room. The hallway was empty except for one student reading a notice on the Drama Club bulletin board, so Emily headed for the nearest stairwell. If she hurried she might still be able to catch Scott before he left school. She skirted around the corner and flew down the stairs two at a time. After three o'clock everyone had to use the main entrance. All the other doors were locked.

She reached the front hallway and stopped to crane her neck. Turning left, then right, she looked through the small groups of students still gathered around their lockers. There was no sign of Scott.

Was she too late? She hoped not as she pushed her way through the wide double doors leading to the quad. Heather's BMW was still parked in front of school. She breathed a sigh of relief. That meant Scott probably hadn't come out yet.

She sat down on the bottom step leading to the front entrance and put her head down on her knees to wait. If she had to wait all day, she was going to talk to Scott and make him believe there was nothing between her and Jonathan but friendship. Then, just maybe, she would tell Scott how she felt about him.

Scott mumbled under his breath and kicked at a pebble as he walked through the rows of cars in the parking lot toward his Jeep. His mother's Buick had been repaired last week, so he finally had his wheels back, and he was glad. He'd hated being chauffeured around by Heather Richardson. All she did was carry on about clothes and jewelry and money. He was happy not to have to listen to her any more. After a while it had gotten so bad he'd started ignoring her, which, as it turned out, was a bigger mistake than agreeing to let her drive him around in the first place.

He slammed his books down on the hood of the Jeep and stuck a hand into his pocket to search for the car keys. Look how she had tricked him into agreeing to take her to the prom. And then telling Emily. . . .

He jerked open the door to the Jeep, snatched his books off the hood, and angrily tossed them onto the backseat. Whenever Scott thought about that afternoon, he got a knot in the middle of his stomach. He'd never been attracted to a girl the way he was to Emily. She was pretty and caring, always thinking of the other guy instead of herself. That's one of the reasons so many people came to her with their problems. And she had liked him, he was sure of it. But now, because of his stupidity, he had ruined any chance for a romance with her. She had already started dating Jonathan Preston, and he had no one to blame but himself.

"Emily?" Elise tapped her tentatively on the shoulder. "What are you doing sitting out here all by yourself?"

Emily quickly brushed the back of her hand across her cheeks before looking up. She didn't want Elise to know she had been crying.

"Em, what's the matter?" Elise asked with concern.

"Nothing," Emily shrugged. She'd been sitting on the step for over half an hour waiting for Scott. "How come you're not at the Burgers' helping Ben and Jonathan pack up the prizes?"

139

"I promised Mrs. Barrie that I would get permission from Mr. Barker to use the school's ovens on carnival night. He was in a meeting so I had to hang around his office until he got out, and the guys said they couldn't wait." Elise dropped her books and sat down on the step. "You sure nothing's wrong?"

Emily stiffened. "I'm sure."

"It's just that you look like you lost your best friend, and I want you to know it's not true. I'm right here beside you," Elise went on, obviously not convinced by Emily's front.

"Thanks." Emily tried to smile.

She drew her knees up to her chest, and leaning forward, clasped her arms around them. Suddenly she couldn't hold it any longer. She turned to Elise, who sat waiting patiently, and searched her mind for the right words to begin. Emily had kept her feelings secret for so long, it was strange to suddenly empty her soul.

"Elise?" she began softly.

"Yes?"

"What would you do if you loved someone, but weren't sure whether or not they cared about you?"

Elise tried not to show her surprise. Was Emily talking about Jonathan?

"I'm not sure," she answered carefully. "What makes you think this person doesn't care about you?"

"Well, he acts really weird around me — like one minute he cares, the next he doesn't. I think he's even jealous of me seeing other boys, but he has a girl friend."

140

She *was* talking about Jonathan! "Have you tried talking to this person? Maybe if you told him how confused you feel. . . ?"

"I just tried, but he ran out of the room." Emily shook her head sadly.

"So, try again. Isn't that what you would tell me to do?" Elise asked. She couldn't believe her best friend had let herself fall in love with Jonathan Preston. He was a terrific guy and all that, but she knew Fiona was still crazy about him, too.

Elise let her breath out slowly. "How long have you been in love with Jonathan?"

Emily's head shot up in surprise. "Jonathan? What does he have to do with this?"

"You're not in love with him?"

Emily shook her head and sighed. "Jonathan Preston and I are friends."

"Then who are we talking about?" Elise was thoroughly confused.

Emily tucked a loose hair behind her ear. She had worn it up today, but after her mad dash to the front entrance, half of it had fallen down. "Scott."

"Scott! Of course." Elise slapped the palm of her hand against her forehead. "I saw you dancing with him at the prom, and you looked awfully happy. I should have guessed you'd gone bonkers over him."

"If it was so obvious, how come you and everyone else think it's Jonathan I'm in love with?"

"Who's everyone else?"

"Scott." Emily swallowed hard. "When he heard me ask Jonathan out tonight, he got all crazy with jealousy and stormed out of the room."

141

"No kidding? I've never known Scott to lose his cool."

"Well, he did today." Emily shook her head sadly. "That's why I'm sitting here. I'm waiting for him to come out of school, then I'm going to make him listen to me."

"What makes you think he's still inside?"

Emily sat straight up. "He has to be. I've been sitting here for the past half hour, and he hasn't come out. Besides Heather's car is still parked in front of the school, and he usually rides home with her." She pointed to the BMW.

"She's probably at pep squad practice, but I think you're wrong about her driving Scott home. I saw him drive up in his Jeep this morning." Elise stood up and glanced over at the parking lot.

"Scott has his own car?"

"Sure. A yellow Jeep. It's great for riding on the beach." Elise sat down again. "And it's gone from the parking lot."

It was Emily's turn to be confused. "But how could he have. . . ."

Elise laughed. "Either you fell asleep, or Scott made it out of school before you took up your post."

"You mean I've been sitting here all this time for nothing?"

"Looks that way." Elise slung an arm around her shoulder. "So how about we head on home? You can fill me in on what's happening between you and Scott as we walk."

Emily gave her friend a nod and got to her feet. Together they walked across the empty quad toward home.

"I don't know if you believe in love at first sight," Emily said, when they got to the next corner. "I didn't until that day I met Scott. It was weird, but the moment I saw him, I was hooked." She snapped her fingers. "Even after you told me you thought he and Heather were a couple, I couldn't turn off my feelings for him."

"Wow! You've really got it bad."

"You're telling me. Elise, I can't stop thinking about him. The time I've spent with him has been wonderful. I feel so alive when I'm with him," Emily rushed on. Now that she had started to talk, the words came pouring out and it felt surprisingly good to confide in someone.

Elise smiled. "I know what you mean. I feel the same way when I'm with Ben. It's great!"

"No, it's painful when you're not sure if the person loves you back."

"Why aren't you sure?"

"Because I can't figure out what kind of relationship he has with Heather." Emily drew in a deep breath. "One minute he acts like he really cares for me — then I find out he's asked *her* to the prom."

"I don't really think Scott is serious about Heather. So what if they went to the prom together? It doesn't mean anything. Didn't you go to the prom with Jonathan?"

"That's different."

"Says who? Judging by the dreamy look on Scott's face when you two were dancing, I'd say he was as crazy about you as you are about him. And anyway, this isn't your style at all. If I were

143

in your position, you know you'd tell me to confront him and set the record straight."

"I know. And that's exactly what I'm planning to do," Emily said when they came to Everett Street. "Remember, that's why I was waiting for him in front of school just now. Tomorrow I'm going to tell Scott how crazy I am about him." She smiled as she turned to head up the hill. "See you tomorrow, Elise, and thanks for letting me bend your ear out of shape."

"Hey, wait a minute." Elise grabbed her by the arm. "Didn't you tell me you asked Jonathan out tonight?"

"I did."

"Well, where are you taking him, and why?"

"I'm taking him to the ballet."

"The ballet? To see Fiona?" Elise stared at her in disbelief.

Emily nodded.

"Does she know what you're planning?"

"Unh-uh," Emily shook her head again. "I'm hoping if Jonathan sees Fiona dance, he'll realize how wrong he was to break up with her. But I didn't want to say anything to Fiona in case it doesn't work out."

Chapter
16

To Emily, Georgetown High looked like an old factory building — large, square, and slightly rundown. It stood between an asphalt yard, surrounded by a chain link fence, and a row of three-story town houses. Tonight, the school yard was being used as a parking lot, and was already half-filled with cars.

Jonathan pulled Big Pink into the yard. "Are you sure this is the right place? It doesn't look like a theater to me," he said, climbing out of the car.

"It's not. It's a school," Emily told him as they walked up the steps.

Inside the metal doors was a large foyer, crowded with people. A young girl wearing a white blouse and dark skirt sat behind a wooden table that held a vase of fresh roses, answering questions and giving out information. When Emily approached her to ask where the box office was, she directed her to a long counter set up on the far side of the foyer.

"I'm going to get the tickets. Be back in a sec." Emily left Jonathan admiring the student sculpture in a display case.

"May I help you?" asked another girl with short, curly hair when Emily stepped up to the counter.

"Yes. My name is Emily Stevens, and there should be two tickets waiting for me."

The girl bent down and pulled out a box marked *Reserved*. "Here you go." She smiled when she came to an envelope with Emily's name on it. "Enjoy the ballet."

"Thanks. Emily walked back to Jonathan. "Ready to go in?"

People were bottled up at the doors leading into the auditorium, but Emily didn't want to wait for the crowd to thin out. She wanted to get Jonathan inside and away from all the posters announcing the ballet before he realized what he was about to watch. He was less likely to bolt once he was in his seat.

"Okay, but what is this thing we're going to see?" Jonathan asked as they moved into the crowd. "It better not be boring like that poetry reading assembly we had last week, or I might fall asleep."

"Relax." Emily took a firm hold of his hand. They were almost at the double-door entrance. "You'll stay awake for this, I promise." If you don't run out first, she added silently. She was beginning to feel very guilty about deceiving Jonathan.

Once they were inside the wide entrance, a boy about Jonathan's age led them to their seats. He held out two programs, which Emily quickly snatched so Jonathan couldn't see them. She was surprised at the turnout. The auditorium was huge — and it was packed. There were even several newspaper photographers crouched in the aisle waiting to take pictures of the performers.

She started moving past the people seated on the aisle and she heard her name being called. "Hey, Em, Over here," Diana cried happily. "I didn't know you were coming." The girls hugged each other. "Is that really Jonathan Preston behind you?"

Emily nodded nervously.

"Hey there," Jeremy reached over to slap Jonathan on the back. "It's great to see you. Does Fiona know you're here to watch her dance?"

Emily felt her throat suddenly tighten. There was no doubt Jonathan knew where he was now. She could feel him stiffen behind her, and she was afraid to turn around and meet his gaze.

"No, uh, she knows nothing about this," Emily told Jeremy quickly. "It was all my idea to bring Jonathan to the ballet." She cleared her throat, then slowly turned around.

For a moment Jonathan just stared at her, his face a mask of stone. Then, with an abrupt turn, he started moving past the person next to him toward the aisle. "Jonathan," she reached out to stop him. "Please don't leave."

He shook her hand loose.

"C'mon, Preston. Stop acting like a jerk!" Jeremy ordered. "You're here already, so why not

147

stay and watch Fiona dance. She can't see you from the stage, and we won't tell her you were here if you don't want us to."

Jonathan shrugged moodily and slunk down into his seat. "I would never have come if I'd known this is where you were taking me." He folded his arms over his chest.

"I know." Emily smiled nervously. "That's why I didn't tell you."

She would have tried explaining more, but just then the lights dimmed and the orchestra struck its first note. A moment later the curtain went up and Emily was instantly mesmerized. The dancers were all wonderful, but no one could compare to Fiona. As she danced the role of Swanilda, she pirouetted around on her toes, with her hands high above her head, and brought oohs and aahs from the young audience. In a pink tutu with her blonde hair swept back from her face, she looked like a miniature ballerina twirling atop a music box.

Even Jonathan couldn't help reacting to the joy that radiated from Fiona as she danced. She was doing more than just demonstrating what she'd learned during years of intense training. She was sharing the love she felt for dancing with her audience.

"How's Jonathan doing?" Diana leaned over to whisper in Emily's ear.

Emily glanced surreptitiously over at him and saw that his eyes were focused intently on Fiona. "I don't know if he'd admit it, but it looks as if he's enjoying himself," she whispered back.

* * *

148

The final curtain came down and Emily turned to Jonathan. When she saw the look of pride and love on his face, she quickly turned away, feeling as if she was eavesdropping on something private.

"Emily?" He turned to her once the applause had died down, and everyone started filing out of the auditorium.

"Hmmm?"

"Thanks." He leaned over and gave her a quick hug.

For a moment Emily just stared at him. "Does this mean what I think it does?"

"What's that?"

"That you're ready to forgive Fiona?"

Jonathan nodded sheepishly. "I guess. Watching her dance tonight made me realize how pig-headed I've been."

Emily let out a sigh of relief. "I knew you would come to your senses sooner or later."

"Yeah, well, I might not have if you hadn't dragged me here tonight. You're something, you know that?"

"You think so?" Emily giggled. "Pass the word around."

"To anyone in particular? Like Scott Phillips?" Jonathan asked seriously.

"Scott!" Emily blanched. "What does he have to do with this?"

"Elise told me he's jealous because you asked me out tonight."

Emily felt a little panicky. "When?"

"When I dropped Ben off at her house this afternoon."

"Oh."

149

"Hey! Don't look so upset." Jonathan put his arm around her. "I'm not going to broadcast it over WKND. I just want you to know I'm willing to assist if you need any help knocking some sense into Scott's head. I owe you one particularly since it's partly my fault he's acting so weird."

Emily looked at him in surprise. "It is?"

"Yeah." Jonathan nodded ruefully. "Scott came to me a couple of times wanting to know what I thought about you. The first time when he started asking me all sorts of dumb questions, I laughed it off. The second time was right after you told him we were going to the prom together, and I was so wrapped up in my own self-pity I didn't realize what he was gettting at. Anyway, I teased him once about how cute I thought you were, and how I'd want to go out with you if I were unattached. That was before I broke up with Fiona."

Emily's face went pale. "And then he heard me asking you out tonight. . . ."

"Poor guy is probably plotting ways to murder me." Jonathan laughed. "I've known Scott for years and I've never seen him act like this before. Must be love."

"What makes you say that?"

"Are you kidding? Why else would he be acting like such a jerk?"

Emily thought about that for a moment. She wanted to believe Jonathan was right. The thought that he was brought a big, open smile to her face.

"Uh, I hate to break this up," Jeremy said loudly from behind them, "but I think it's time we left. Diana and I want to get to the stage door before Fiona comes out. We told her we'd drive her home," he added for Jonathan's benefit.

Jonathan stood up quickly. "Sorry old buddy." He smiled. "You've been relieved of that duty. *I* intend to drive Fiona home."

Jeremy's mouth fell open. "Anyone ever tell you that you change colors faster than a chameleon?"

Jonathan plopped his hat on his head. "On occasion. Look, do you mind if Emily rides home with you? I want to meet Fiona by the stage door — alone." He looked at Jeremy before turning to Emily. "That's okay with you, isn't it?"

"No problem." Emily reached up to put her hand on Jonathan's shoulder. "Just be sure to tell Fiona I said she lived up to her promise."

As Fiona and a few of the other cast members stepped out the stage door, a group of young girls waiting in the hallway descended on them asking for their autographs.

"Someday I'm going to dance just like you," a little girl sang out when Fiona handed back her mimeographed program.

"Me, too," said another young voice.

Fiona bent down to hug both girls. "Thank you," she said smiling. She was very moved.

She had loved dancing for the kids tonight. They were such an enthusiastic audience, and now just looking at their faces as they stood waiting for her autograph, she knew she had made the right choice when she agreed to dance in *Coppelia*.

When the last little girl stepped forward, she handed Fiona a single red rose. "The man over there said to give this to you." She pointed toward the main entrance.

Fiona looked up and saw a familiar form leaning against the wall. "Jonathan." She blinked once to make sure it was really him.

He looked so handsome standing there with his hands stuffed into the pockets of his jeans and his Indiana Jones hat shoved back on his dark blond hair.

He tipped his hat and smiled.

Fiona clutched the rose in both hands and moved toward him slowly. She felt shy and a little nervous, and not at all sure what she would say to him. It was like being on a first date.

"Hi," he said when she stopped before him.

"Hi, yourself," she answered shyly. "Did you see the ballet?"

Jonathan nodded. "You were great."

"Thank you." Fiona shifted her gaze away from his face and intently studied the floor. "And thanks for the rose."

"Glad you like it." He gave her an odd smile. "I swiped it from the front table."

"I don't care. It's beautiful." She lifted it up to her nose and inhaled deeply.

"Uh, well, if you're ready we can go. I mean, I'm here to drive you home," Jonathan explained.

Fiona felt her heart skip a beat.

He led the way to his car and they both climbed into the front seat. There was an awkward silence as he reached forward to start the engine. Then he hesitated and turned to Fiona.

"I've missed you."

She looked at Jonathan for a moment, then flung herself into his arms. It was what she had been waiting to hear ever since this terrible mix-up had started. She pressed her cheek against the soft leather of his jacket and smelled the familiar scent of the spicy aftershave she'd always loved.

"Oh, Jonathan. I've missed you, too." They clung together like that for a moment, Jonathan running one hand through Fiona's hair over and over again. She noticed his eyes never left her face, even when she finally pulled away slightly.

He took both her hands in his. "Can you ever forgive me for acting like such a creep? It was so dumb. I mean, here I was blaming you for being so caught up in your dancing when I was just as hung up on making the prom a success."

Fiona looked at him. His gray eyes were full of remorse, and she could tell how hard it was for him to apologize.

"Sometimes I guess I get so wrapped up in what I'm doing, I forget that other people, like you, have things that are important to them, too. What I mean is, if dancing in *Coppelia* was more important to you than going to the prom, I should have understood."

He took Fiona in his arms again and hugged her tightly, as if he were trying to squeeze out any bad feelings that were left inside her. She rested her head on his shoulder and closed her eyes. Being in his arms again made her feel so safe and warm. When they separated, Jonathan looked into Fiona's eyes.

"When I saw you dance tonight, all the hurt and anger I'd been carrying around since Laurie's party suddenly disappeared. You looked terrific up there on stage." He touched her chin lightly. "And your smile, it was so full of love — like it is now. I guess I'm going to have to get used to the fact that you have two loves — me and dancing," he teased.

Fiona smiled into his gray eyes. "I'm so sorry I had to miss the prom, Jonathan."

"I know that now. As for the prom" — he laced his fingers through hers — "it was a real success. But you and I can dance together any time."

Fiona leaned over to kiss him. As their lips met in a sweet, gentle kiss that sent a tingling sensation all the way down to her toes, she thought that she had never loved Jonathan more than at this moment.

Chapter
17

Emily wasn't taking any chances. Instead of running around school looking for Scott, she decided to wait for him by his Jeep. It was almost two-thirty. Emily knew she shouldn't have walked out of school before the final bell. But when Madame Fontaine, her eighth-period French teacher, had sent her to the office with a note for the school custodian, instead of going back upstairs for the last few minutes of class she decided to leave. That way she wouldn't miss Scott.

All she could think about was talking to Scott and finding out why he had acted so strange yesterday. She couldn't stand not knowing how he felt about her. She intended to find out and end her confusion and frustration once and for all.

She tilted her face up to catch the warmth of the sun's rays and leaned against the Jeep. No one was going to be working on the carnival this afternoon because of the baseball game. Kennedy was playing Carrolton High and most of the student body would be going to cheer on the Cardinals. She pushed a wisp of hair off her forehead and rolled up the sleeves of her pink sweater.

A few minutes later, a small cloud passed overhead, temporarily blocking the sun. As Emily lowered her head, she spotted Scott taking long strides across the parking lot. There was no mistaking the slope of his wide shoulders and the thick blond hair that rested just over the collar of his rugby shirt. Her heart started beating like a tiny snare drum.

"Emily!" Scott drew his brows together questioningly. "What are you doing hanging around the parking lot? Aren't you going to the game?"

Emily stood up straight and lifted her eyes to meet Scott's. "No. I have to talk to you," she said firmly. "I have to know why you reacted that way yesterday when I asked Jonathan to the ballet."

"So that's where you went." Scott stuck his hands in his pockets and leaned against the door of the Jeep.

"Yes. I took him to see Fiona dance. I was hoping it would make him realize it was a mistake to break up with her."

Scott looked confused. "Why would you want to do that?"

A cool breeze blew across the lot and Emily hugged herself to ward off the chill. She hadn't worn a jacket. "Because Fiona is my friend. And so is Jonathan. I wanted to get them back together again."

"Well, I think it worked. I saw them together in the hallway before lunch." Scott turned to lean his arms on top of the hood.

Emily walked over to stand next to him. "I know it did. So tell me, were you jealous that I was going out with Jonathan?"

"What do you think?"

"I don't know. Whenever I let myself think you might care about me, I wind up looking like a fool, as though I've really misjudged your actions."

Scott looked at her over his shoulder. "That makes two of us."

"What do you mean?"

"I thought you realized how I felt about you that afternoon in the student activities room. How could you have thought I was interested in anyone else, Emily?"

Scott turned to face her and she could see the sincerity in his eyes.

Emily shifted. "How was I supposed to know? I thought you were still going out with Heather."

"Going out!" Scott looked shocked. "Heather and I aren't even friends!"

"But you went to the prom together, and I've seen you in her car lots of times."

Scott laughed. "Sure, I took her to the prom, but *she* asked *me*! She sort of . . . tricked me into it. . . . I don't know how, exactly. . . . As for riding in Heather's BMW, we live on the same block. My mother's Buick was being repaired, so she was using my Jeep to get to work. When Heather saw me waiting for the school bus, she offered to drive me until my mother's car was fixed."

A surge of joy shot through Emily at Scott's explanation. "Then there's nothing between you and Heather?"

Still leaning against his Jeep, Scott reached for Emily's hand. "No," he said, running a finger lightly over her palm. "Do you believe me?"

"I believe you," Emily said softly.

Scott pulled her gently to him and gathered her up in his arms. "I love you, Emily Stevens. I guess I have ever since the day we jogged in the rain."

"Why didn't you tell me sooner? It would have made things a lot easier. I think that was the same day I fell in love with you." She leaned against the length of his body and reached up to clasp her arms around his neck.

"I thought you would know when I kissed you. Isn't that what kisses are for? I hope you don't go around kissing everyone like that." He paused and chuckled before going on. "When you wouldn't let me explain about Heather and told me you were going to the prom with Jonathan, I figured you weren't available anyway."

"For someone who's always giving out advice, I sure made a mess out of things, huh? Maybe we should start over."

"Now that sounds like a great idea. I'll drive you home so you can change into your jogging clothes. Then I'll meet you in the park by the water fountain."

"If you insist," Emily said.

"I do, but before we go anywhere. . . ." Scott leaned closer and kissed her gently on the lips.

The rest of the week passed by in a blur for Emily. She and Scott spent every free moment they had together. They even managed to meet between classes a few times a day. It was now the morning of the carnival, and the juniors were busy putting the final touches on the game booths.

"I hope you guys don't mind if I split as soon as I finish blowing up these balloons." Jonathan sat cross-legged on the floor beside Emily. "This afternoon is Fiona's last performance, and I promised her I'd be there."

"How many times have you seen *Coppelia* now?" Scott asked. He was standing near Jonathan on a stepstool, taping red and gold crepe-paper streamers onto the kissing booth. The gazebolike structure sat in the center of the gym, and had different-sized cardboard hearts pasted all over it.

"Four," Jonathan answered, his face glowing as he handed Emily another balloon to tack onto the dart board.

"What you mean is that you've been to the ballet every night this week, right?" Emily teased. She couldn't believe this was the same Jonathan who'd been sulking around school for the past two weeks. His whole body seemed to glow with a new kind of energy. She pushed a thumb tack through the knot in the balloon and stuck it on the dart board. "That's what I call true love."

"Look who's talking," Jonathan shot back. "I

haven't seen you without Scott since Tuesday. And don't try telling me it's because of the carnival," he added quickly. "I happen to have noticed the two of you huddled together behind the stairwell before study period."

Elise walked up to them, dressed in painter's overalls and holding a paintbrush. "Mind if I ask a question?"

"Go ahead," Emily said. She was grateful for the interruption. She'd been embarrassed to learn Jonathan had seen her and Scott behind the stairwell.

Elise put her free hand on her hip. "Did we or did we not decide to have the boys take turns working the kissing booth?"

Emily looked at Ben standing behind Elise with a scowl on his face. She could tell he wasn't too thrilled about the decision. "Elise is right." She picked up her clipboard and flipped it to the shift schedules. "Let's see, I've got you down for the second-to-last shift."

"No way!" Ben looked stricken.

"Don't worry, Mr. Wizard." Elise laughed. "I'll be watching to make sure no one takes advantage of you." She tapped him on the nose with the handle of her paintbrush, and walked off.

Jonathan and Scott took one look at Ben, and broke up laughing.

"What's so funny?" Emily smiled wickedly. "The two of you are also scheduled to work the kissing booth."

Their laughter stopped abruptly. "Who's going to want to kiss us?" Jonathan asked.

"Oh, I can think of a number of girls who would like a chance to kiss the student activities director. And as for you, Scott, Heather Richardson might buy a kiss." If I give her a chance, Emily thought to herself. She wasn't going to let on now, but she intended to monopolize Scott during his twenty-minute shift in the kissing booth.

Chapter
18

The gym was already crowded when Fiona walked in with Jonathan. She paused in the doorway to admire the colorful game booths and large banner strung across the back wall. Music blared from the speakers Brian Pierson had rigged up on either side of the makeshift stage. and those students who weren't already waiting in line to play a game were dancing at the far end of the gym.

"Hey, you guys. You're late!" Emily came up to them with a big grin on her face She was wearing a funky turquoise top and beige miniskirt that showed off her great legs. Scott was right beside her, his arm casually draped across her shoulder.

"The gym looks fabulous!" Fiona's eyes were shining with excitement.

"You can say that again." Jonathan scanned the colorful streamers hanging from the ceiling before turning to Scott and Emily. "I'm impressed. When I left this afternoon the gym looked like a tornado had swept through it."

"If I remember correctly you cut out pretty early," Emily teased.

"Yeah, but I had a good reason." Jonathan slipped his hand into Fiona's. She turned to look at him with shining eyes.

"You'll get no argument here." Emily gave them both a big smile.

Jonathan laughed. "Thanks. Now fill me in. How's it going?"

"Look around for yourself." Scott grinned. "The carnival only started a few minutes ago, and already this place is going wild."

"What he means," Emily cut in, "is that the seniors seem to be having a good time."

"Yeah. Just look at the size of the crowd around the Rambo booth." Scott directed Jonathan's attention to the group of seniors cheering on Bart Einerson as he threw wet sponges at Mr. Baylor. "Bart hasn't missed once."

"I hope old eagle-eyes doesn't decide to get back at us on Monday." Fiona bit her lip. "I've got study hall with him third period."

"Let's just hope he dries off by then," Jonathan said as another wet sponge hit Mr. Baylor square in the face. The crowd started cheering as the teacher stepped back to wipe his face with a towel.

"What kind of prizes are you giving out for the sponge toss?" Fiona asked, laughing.

"Everything you could possibly think of," a familiar voice rang out from behind.

Emily whirled around and saw Elise holding an armful of colored pencils, T-shirts, and stuffed animals. "Where are you going with all those?"

"Ben needs them for the sponge toss. He's running out of prizes."

"Already? You sure he isn't giving them away?" Jonathan plucked a green frog from her arms.

"Put that back, Preston," Elise said with mock severity. "If you want the frog you're going to have to win it."

Jonathan dropped the frog in her arms and laughed. "It's a deal." He turned to Emily. "What's my schedule for the next few shifts?"

Emily looked down at her clipboard. "Let's see." She flipped over the top page and glanced at her watch. "Okay, I've got you and Fiona working the dart game from nine to nine-thirty. Then you've both got a half hour off before Fiona goes to the water-pistol range and you report to the kissing booth."

"Great!" Jonathan smiled. "We'll see you later." He wandered off with Fiona in search of a game to play.

Scott put his arm around Emily. "I'd better get over to the ring toss before I'm tempted to play a few games myself." He gave her a quick kiss before running off.

Emily walked over to the sponge toss booth with Elise, and after making sure they weren't going to run out of prizes, spent the next fifteen minutes walking around the gym. She smiled when she spotted Phoebe and Chris coming out of the fun house, their hair covered with spaghetti streamers. But when she caught sight of Kim Barrie carrying a goldfish in a bowl, the smile on her face turned to an ear-to-ear grin.

"Look what Woody just won for me," Kim said.

"Talent . . . that's all it takes." Woody beamed.

"Sure." Kim laughed. "That and twelve tries." She turned to Emily.

"But you got your goldfish, didn't you?" Woody said.

"You bet I did." Kim smiled at him affectionately. "Now all I have to do is think up a name."

"You're nuts," Woody said. playfully rumpling her hair. "Who ever heard of naming a goldfish?"

"What's so silly about that?" Kim asked. "Haven't you ever heard of Mickey Mouse, Donald Duck, and," she smiled wickedly. "Woody Woodpecker? I'm just adding Greta Goldfish to the list."

"In that case we'd better hit some of the other booths before you go completely wacko," he said, glancing around the gym.

"Fine with me." Kim winked at Emily and they wandered off arm-in-arm.

Emily watched Kim and Woody disappear behind the kissing booth before continuing on her rounds. Everyone really seemed to be enjoying themselves. Now that the carnival was in full swing, each booth had a line of people waiting, and many of the students were clutching prizes they had won.

At nine-thirty the music stopped, and Jonathan stepped onto the make-shift stage. "Attention, everyone!" he called into the microphone Ben handed him. Gradually the gym quieted down, and he continued, "I hate to interrupt your fun, but I want to welcome you to the first Senior Carnival ever! I also want to explain why we decided to throw this event for you guys."

There was a hush in the crowd.

"There are two reasons, actually. First, the junior class wanted to show you seniors that the Rollerthon wasn't just a fluke. We lowly juniors can organize things — without your help. Secondly" — he paused dramatically — ". . . we wanted to do something special for all of you, so you'll remember how terrific we are after you leave Kennedy High."

The gym immediately erupted with shouts and catcalls, Woody's voice being the loudest.

"I take it you agree we're the greatest!" Jonathan said and was rewarded with more catcalls and hisses.

"Get off the stage, Preston, and let us get back to our fun," Bart Einerson called out.

"Okay, end of speech." Jonathan started to put down the microphone.

"Wait!" Phoebe shouted from where she and a few other seniors were huddled in an impromtu conference.

A moment later Chris Austin stepped forward. "The seniors have asked me to say a word on their behalf." She climbed onto the stage.

"As their representative," she spoke into the microphone, "let me say thank you to all of you juniors. The senior class," her eyes swept the crowd, but her glance lingered on her friends: Phoebe, Michael, Sasha, Kim, and Woody, who all stood beaming, "thinks you guys are really terrific and did one heck of a job setting up this carnival!"

There was a burst of applause.

Chris held up her hand. "Wait! I want to add that while it's still hard to believe that we seniors will be graduating in a few weeks, after tonight, we are confident we'll be leaving Kennedy High in good hands."

Ted Mason leapt to his feet, shouting and stomping his approval. Molly, his girl friend, and Brenda Austin stood next to him clapping.

Emily swelled with pride. This last week had been the best in her entire life. First everything had been straightened out with Scott, and now the carnival was going full-swing and everyone seemed to be loving it. In her wildest dreams, she never imagined it would be such a success.

The music started up again and Jonathan jumped off the stage. "Since we're all free for the next half hour, what do you say we slip into the cafeteria and sample some of Mrs. Barrie's cooking?" He looked from Fiona to Emily and Scott. "I don't know about you guys, but I could sure use something to nibble on."

"You two go ahead," Scott told him. "Emily and I will catch up with you later. There's something I've got to discuss with her first."

With a flick of his head Scott gestured for Emily to follow him out of the gym. It was a perfect spring night. The air was fresh and crisp, and the sky shimmered with thousands of brilliant stars.

"Guess you're wondering why I dragged you

out here, huh?" Scott said, nuzzling his cheek against her hair as they walked through the damp grass over to the bleachers.

"Uh-huh." Emily sighed and wrapped her arm more tightly around his waist.

"I just wanted to be alone with you for a few minutes."

"I'm glad. Me, too."

"The carnival's a huge success, but noisy."

"I know."

They climbed up to the top bleacher, and snuggled together looking up at the star-filled sky.

"It's quiet and peaceful out here." Scott slipped his arm through Emily's. "And you know what else?" He rested his forehead on hers and stared into her eyes.

"What?"

"It's the perfect place for me to practice for my shift in the kissing booth." He cupped her face in his hands and kissed her gently on the mouth. "How was that?"

Emily gave a mischievous smile. "Not bad, but it could use improvement."

"Okay." He kissed her again.

"Better." Emily started to laugh.

"More?" He slid his arms around to the small of her back, and pressed her tightly to his chest.

"Mmmmmm." Emily reached her arms around his neck and closed her eyes. But when his lips met hers this time there was nothing funny about his kiss. Just a special warmth that spread from him to her and back again.

Coming Soon . . .
Couples #23
BYE BYE LOVE

The bonfire was raging on the banks of the Potomac, and Phoebe stood in the silent circle of seniors gathered around it, hugging a shadowy bundle to her chest. The round of graduation parties was over, and it was time for the passing on ceremony. During the graduation night bonfire at Potomac Park, each senior would toss a prized possession — one that symbolized the best of their life at Kennedy High — into the flames.

Now, someone, Woody or Bart, began humming the Kennedy Fight Song, softly and slowly. Soon everyone joined in. It sounded so sad and meaningful, more like a dirge than a call to action. First Peter stepped up to the fire carrying a record album. The cover was worn and frayed, and in the flickering light Phoebe made out the title and stifled a gasp: Springsteen's *Born in the U.S.A.* Peter tossed it into the flames, and Phoebe watched in horror as the cardboard cover wrinkled up, baring the melting black disc inside. Ted

169

stepped up next. From the circle of juniors behind her, Phoebe heard a loud sniff. It was Molly. Phoebe focused her attention back on Ted in time to see him throw a baseball into the flames. "He hit his first home run with that!" Molly whispered in the dark. Chris sacrificed her favorite pair of penny loafers; Monica, an old stuffed yellow dog with one eye missing; Bart, his Stetson; Woody, his best red suspenders; Laurie, her heart-shaped plastic Candy Hearts pocketbook; and Michael, a warped but beloved old bow for his cello.

Then Brenda stepped out of the shadows, and Phoebe watched her slowly approach the fire. For a moment Phoebe feared Brenda was going to take off the beautiful turquoise earring Brad had given her and throw it in, but instead Brenda pulled off the small triangle cloth, tied loosely about her throat. Just before Brenda dropped it into the blaze, Phoebe recognized it as Brad's worn blue bandanna.

Then it was Phoebe's turn. She stepped forward cautiously, holding back tears. She squeezed her bundle tightly before giving it up. This was something that couldn't be undone. She looked up and caught Michael's eye. He was standing across the fire from her, an encouraging smile on his face. Phoebe forced herself to keep her eyes open. Then with a brave "Whoop," she hurled her worn pink overalls into the blaze. "Goodbye!" she whispered.